PLEASE DON'T

S. A. FANNING

Immortal Works LLC
1505 Glenrose Drive
Salt Lake City, Utah 84104
Tel: (385) 202-0116

Cover Art by Bukovero Cover Design
https://bukovero.com

ISBN 978-1-953491-26-8 (Paperback)
ASIN B09JPGJ12J (Kindle)

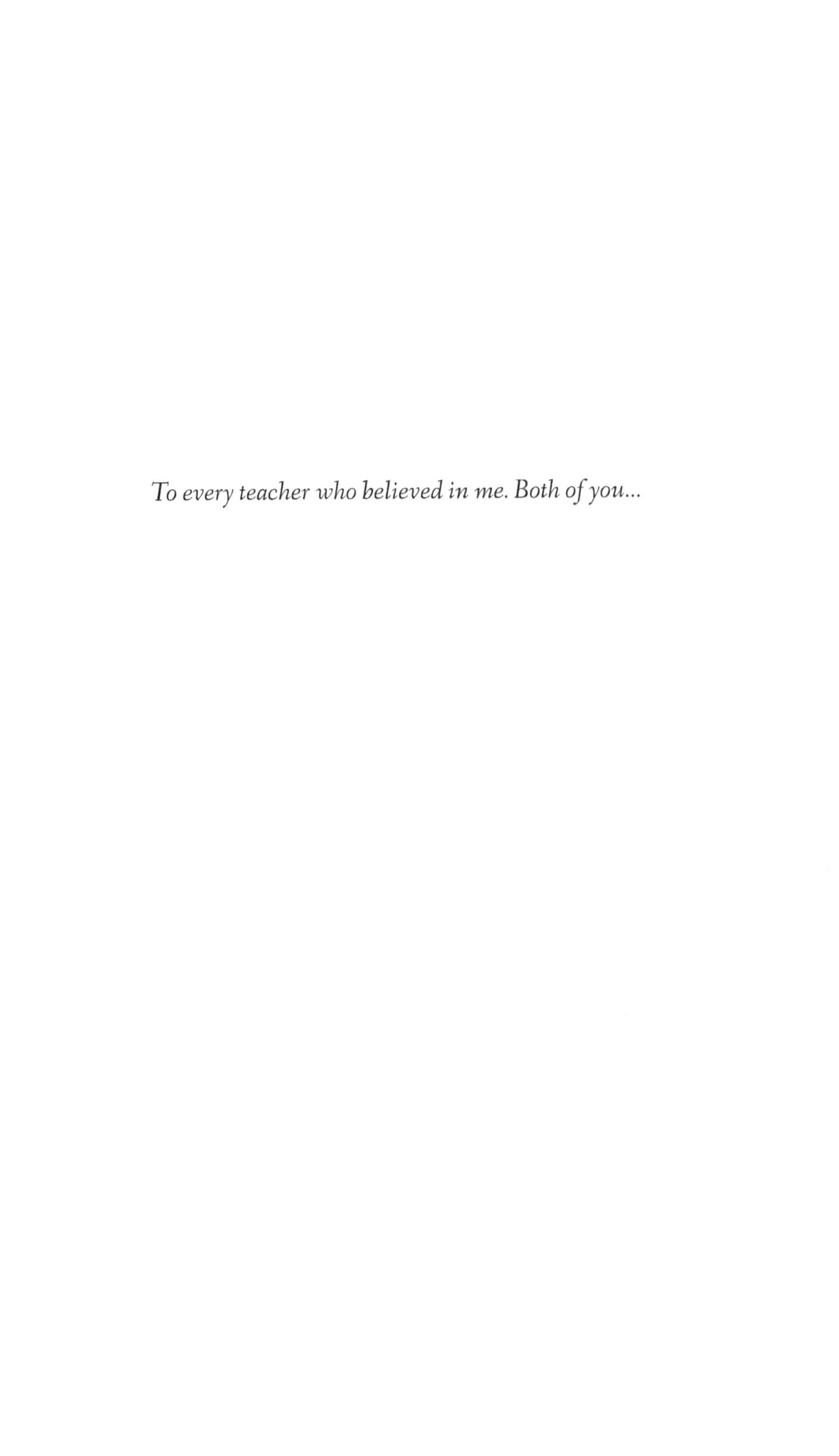

To every teacher who believed in me. Both of you...

1

I find the letter in the mailbox, tucked between a colorful assortment of bills and threats. Its formality stands out; the envelope is thick and textured, stamped with the official town decal. A slightly askew address label in some no-nonsense font bears my home address.

I'm sweaty, my VIRGIL'S LAWN CARE t-shirt sticks to my back as a familiar dread sinks to my stomach. My hands tremble as I fiddle with the edges of the envelope, my heart *thump-thumping* in my ears as I tear it open and face my fate. Four neat little paragraphs from the Woodberry Board of Education, including a time and date for the hearing on my status to determine whether I will be allowed to attend Garner High next year.

Dear Mrs. Reams,

While no legal action will be taken against Nathanial Reams, the Woodberry School District will recommend that he be expelled from Garner High School.

Right to the point, those guys. I gloss over it impatiently, skipping down the reasons listed. *Truancy...violation of school rules...assault.*

Basically, it states I'm an all-around menace.

...For the safety of students and faculty due to actions and behavior listed (here it cites page numbers and sections of the student handbook).

The board of education will meet on Monday, July 22, at 6pm in the municipal office. This issue on the agenda is scheduled for approximately 6:25 pm. At this meeting of the school board, you (and/or anyone you choose to represent or assist you, at your own expense) may appear and present whatever information you believe is relevant to the recommendation to expel.

This is where I stop reading. The school board is assuming I will be able to rouse my mother from bed, get her dressed and presentable, keep her sober and coherent—or upright enough to convince them she is. The board is assuming a lot.

Inside I find the regular messes. Dirty dishes, a half-eaten pop tart. A spread of saltines and cheese squares on the counter. My feet crunch over the scatter of crumbs on the floor where a trail of cotton balls, the kind from a pill bottle, lead to the trash. Balled up receipts, lipstick, pens, a key ring, jewelry—it looks like someone took a purse and shook it out all over the kitchen.

I clean the mess and start on dinner. While waiting for this letter, I've done a lot of thinking about my options—about breaking a promise and coming forward about what really happened at school. But whenever I'm tempted to do that, I hear two words in my head.

"Please don't..."

The first words Molly Martinez ever said to me.

Her voice cracked into a whisper when she said it. Her glassy red eyes, hiding behind strands of black hair that had fallen over her face, darted towards the door. It wasn't until then, as she eyed her escape, that I realized I'd never paid much attention to Molly.

Please don't *what?* I wanted to say. But I knew what she didn't want me to do or say. It wasn't hard to figure out. Not when she flung her book bag over her shoulder and scrambled off without looking back. When she left me alone with nothing to do but face what I had done.

Our chemistry teacher sat slumped over, groaning and holding his face, droplets of blood dripping to the floor. Later I'd find out his nose was broken in two places. But hey, I'd promised.

Please don't.

So I don't. I never said a thing to anyone. Except Molly. I begged and pleaded with Molly Martinez. I even got her a job cutting grass with me to help her family with the bills. But she never budged, never came forward.

Now I'm expelled.

I call Mom down for dinner. She slips into her seat across from me and curls her lip at the plate of chicken tenders and mac and cheese I've set in front of her. Not exactly black-tie scallops, but I'm working on a budget here.

I roll my eyes, because I'm not in the mood for this, for any of it. "Just eat, Mom."

She wiggles her nose, takes up her fork and starts picking around. The mac and cheese is runny, pooling into the chicken. I had to use water because I forgot to pick up milk. Just looking at it makes me want to throw the plate against the wall.

Mom must be thinking the same thing. She closes her eyes and whispers, "Yuck."

With her plate pushed to the center of the table, she covers her mouth with her napkin. I grip my fork tighter. Usually I can deal with it, but today, after the letter...

Her makeup looks as though it's been swiped on by a three-year-old. It's smeared across her cheeks, her lips, a glop on her eyelashes. Her shoulders sag. She sighs. "You haven't said a word about my hair."

I grab the back of my neck. This woman changed my diapers,

wiped my butt, spoon fed me meals so I wouldn't starve. We have home videos, somewhere, if she hasn't destroyed them, of her feeding me when I was a baby. *Open up the hatch, Nat, here comes the carrots.*

I tell myself that person is still in there, knocking around somewhere. But I don't see her at the table. Haven't seen her in a while. I try to move things along.

"Sorry, I'm just tired, from work, cleaning up...whatever happened in the kitchen. Then cooking dinner."

"Nat, you sound like your father."

She has to know it's the worst thing she can say. I look away, tell myself to hold it together. Not to blame her for how my life sucks. Not to ask her how she can sit there and be so selfish.

Instead, I start in on my tenders while she puffs out her cheeks and looks around the room. It's all I can do not to slam my fork down on the table. Like Dad used to do.

Mom is all about Mom these days. She fashions herself a playwright, and when she's not drinking, she's busy clicking away on my laptop—the one Dad bought me a few years ago. At least it keeps her busy. Besides, if you try to argue with her she assumes the role of misunderstood writer, as played by mischievous toddler.

She's getting huffy, and I'm half expecting her to stick her tongue out at me. I set my fork down, gently, and make a point of considering her hair. Peroxide blonde, the hue of toxic sludge, sheared with a nail file or dull scissors. If she's going for the look of woman on the run, she's nailed it. I take a breath and try again. "Mom, your hair really does look nice."

Her eyes light up, animated. She cocks her head to the side, stroking her hack job hair. "Really. It's not too short?"

"No, it goes well with your, um, outfit."

She looks down. "You think?"

Today's theme is festive. Palm trees. She has a dozen or more of these scrubs, and it messes with my head because it reminds me of better times when she really was a nurse and went to work. When everything was, what? Normal?

When Dad took off Mom kept up with her appearance for a while. At least she wasn't gnawing off her hair and swiping on makeup. Months, a year passed, and I guess she thought Dad might be coming back—we both did—so she still wore normal clothes. Then, at some point after that, she said screw it. This is the result.

"Has um, Gary seen it?"

She grins. "Stop it."

Gary-the-Editorial-Guy is an older, early to mid-fifties dude from Mom's writer group. He wears brown polyester suits, the kind found at your local Goodwill. He's a nice enough guy, I guess. And he's hopelessly incapable of hiding his crush on my mom.

Seeing her smile makes me chuckle. I get back to my food. Mom crosses her arms and remains on hunger strike. This week I've only seen her eat yogurt and Fig Newtons. It's what I mean about having a toddler in the house, one who drinks all night and never blows out the candles.

I clean my plate and I tear into Mom's portion. I eat both of our dinners and wonder what we'll do tomorrow night. I get paid this Friday so at least I can pick up toilet paper and stop using fast food napkins. I can't tell you what Mom is using. Maybe she has her own personal stash.

Done sulking, Mom stands and drifts over to the fridge, humming a show tune. She fills a plastic cup with wine and shuffles to the den. I sit at the table, alone, wondering what I could have said differently.

I wanted to talk about my hearing, or what we're going to do about our tax delinquency, which is up to something like twelve-grand, last I checked. I even left the school board letter face up on the counter, its official letterhead screaming out its importance. But again, Mom is all about Mom these days.

I go back and forth between wanting to help her and hating her for not snapping out of it. Between wanting to leave and wanting to stay. I ride the waves of guilt and blame. When I'm at work, I do nothing but worry about her, when I'm home, I just want to leave.

Like Dad did.

Pick up the plates. Rinse off the runny cheese. Go make sure she's okay. Just like last night and the night before that. But tonight, the sink is too full, the counters are too sticky with wine and fig crumbs. It's too much.

Let the flies have their fun, I'm done.

Upstairs, I sprawl out on my bed, ready to indulge in my secret pastime. I pull out my phone and open the browser. There it waits for me. I don't even have to search for it. One swipe and it's there at my fingertips.

One More Makes Four!

It's not a math tutorial, but a parenting blog. One so choked full of product placement it sometimes crashes my phone. The usual onslaught of advertisements bombards me, and I have to close out windows and hunt for any real content, which is bogged down by sponsorships and branding. The side bars feature soaps, shampoos, diapers, clothing, apps, social media links, books, giveaways, contests, and on and on and on and on as far as I can scroll. Eventually, I find what I'm looking for: a picture of the family—Dad's family.

They pose with other bloggers and consultants. Everyone is all smiles, and it's hard to tell what the actual point of any of this is in the first place.

It's a cruel form of self-torture, reading about Kristen—my dad's wife, blogger extraordinaire—and how she feels about "mommyhood", as she calls it. In yesterday's post, she ranted about how hard it is to find decent free educational apps. And wherever there is a heartwarming story about her daughter, rest assured that lurking beneath her dribble is some sort of product placement. She reviews anything and has no problem using her kid, my dad, or the yet-to-be-born child to boost clicks. She's kind of a pimp like that.

I devour her latest post, complete with a picture of the happy family at the dinner table playing a board game. My dad is all teeth, giving a big thumbs-up. It's almost weird now to think about him as my dad, even stranger how the blonde chunkster is sort of my sister. While my mom has transformed into...whatever she's become, it seems Kristen has created a new version of Dan Reams—the ultimate family-dude. Tall, a bit of silver sliding in at the temples, but otherwise his hair is thick and stylish. He's kind of soft in the middle, but you can tell Kristen runs him to death. *Sponsored by Nike!*

I pore over some pictures of the family cooking out, zooming in and studying the details. Dan Reams wearing a new grilling apron by *Grill Masters™*. I stare at his face. Our bone structure is similar. No one could look at his picture then look at me and not tell. We have the same jawline, nose, blue eyes, and broad shoulders. The more I study the pixels, the harder it is to figure out. The harder it is to let it go.

It would be so much easier to swallow if the guy was a drunk or in prison. That, I could accept if not understand. If he was just some loser who didn't want his family, maybe I'd be okay with it. Maybe I wouldn't be. But he's not a loser, he's like Dad of the Year. And it sort of kills me a little bit.

I can't even remember how I found this blog. I think I was Google searching his name and stumbled upon it. It's got thousands of followers. It's been viewed nearly half a million times. And I've been stopping by two or three times a day for the past six months. Again, probably not the healthiest habit, but hey, neither is pimping your kids for sponsors, right?

What the blog fails to mention is how Dan Reams took off for Indiana nearly four years ago, leaving behind a three hundred-thousand-dollar house and an eight-year-old Honda. Maybe he figured a house and car was enough, because he doesn't pay a dime of child support or call or write or even remember us for all I know. And Mom is either too proud or too delusional to try to get anything out of him, which means she's delinquent—in more ways than one—on property taxes, utilities, homeowner association fees, credit cards, and I'm sure a slew of other bills I don't even know about. Which leaves me here, waiting for something to happen.

For a while it was easy to ignore. My parents' fighting. Mom's drinking. Dad leaving. Bills piling up in the mailbox as I went about life like nothing was wrong. School. Basketball. Girlfriend. Parties. Anything to not think about what was happening at home. But it did happen. They decided not to be the parents I knew. People change, I get it, but when Dad quit the marriage and Mom quit life, it felt like they both quit me.

I close the app and sift through my contacts. Nearly one hundred of them, all ghosts after everything went down at school. I think about work and life and Molly Martinez. How these days I have no distractions, nothing to keep me from worrying. I think about whether I should even tell Molly about the hearing. I wonder if she knows what I gave up or what my future has become.

Suddenly I feel so alone it makes me shiver.

2

Molly is a no-show at work the next morning. Virgil and I sweat it out at the Willows, an apartment complex that's all hills and roots and parking lots with little islands and curbs and push mowing. By lunchtime Virgil is grumbling. He's pushing three hundred pounds, so any extra work makes him grumble.

We're finishing up our gas station hot dogs. Two for me, three for him. "She didn't even call," Virgil says between either burps or hiccups, it's hard to tell.

Molly is all of five feet, maybe a hundred pounds, but she can work a push-mower like it's nothing. She shows me up all the time, loading and unloading the trailer, doing the grunt work, while I'm habitually late and never stick around to make up my hours.

"She's never missed a day, Virg. I'm sure she has a good reason. I'll swing by her place on the way home."

He cuts a look my way, sweat still draining off his forehead. This is my second summer with Virgil, and I've never seen him wear anything besides overalls. His arms are covered with tattoos, all in various stages of fading into his leathery skin and buried under a thicket of fur. He's shorter than me, but I always feel small around him. Still, under all his gruff he's a softy, and I know from experience I'm dangerously close to suffering through another Uncle Virgil sweaty moment.

"I'd be careful doing that."

"Uh, okay."

He snorts. "Yeah, okay nothing. She's a good-looking *chica*. Might have some *esse's* come looking for you."

I turn to walk away. "I appreciate your concern."

"Yeah, okay." He snorts. But seeing how I'm not getting worked up, he drops it.

Virgil's casual racism used to offend me. I mean, it still does, but today I don't have the energy.

In the truck we ride a while in silence, only Virgil's constant talk radio and the rattle of ice in his 54oz gut buster soda occupy the cab. He's still roasting, his face swamped with sweat even though I did all the push mowing. He looks at me, the road, then me again. *Here we go.*

"You doing okay? With your folks and all?"

Exactly *one time* I made the mistake of telling Virgil about my dad, and now he's constantly asking me about my "folks and all." Not only that, he's also part of Mom's fan club. Like Gary, he's crushing hard. He told me once how she needed someone who's been there. I don't know where exactly "there" is, but I'm guessing it's not a beach resort.

I give him a nod. "Yeah, it's good."

He starts in with the whole, "if you ever need to talk," thing. But talking to Virg is like pulling the lever on a random cliché generator. *Life sucks. Nothing comes easy. Can't choose family.* Oh, and who can forget his favorite, *Suck it up, kiddo.* I like Virg and all, he means well, but the guy should stick to cleaning carburetors.

The afternoon drags. It's bad enough with a three-man crew, being how Virgil is too cheap to hire a fourth guy, but with two it's brutal. We get through the day, and after I finish unloading the trailer I figure, screw it, I'm going to go check on Molly.

I used to tell myself it was her fault, my predicament. But it's not. Even if I'd never walked into the chem lab that afternoon and saw what I saw, I probably would have ended up punching Mr. Meyers in the face anyway. Then again, if I'd never rolled Meyers, I'd be playing AAU ball right now, not cutting grass with Virgil for eight bucks an hour.

In the sun visor lies my mom's antique compact disc collection. I shove in the Al Green CD, and soon I'm singing along with *Tired of Being Alone,* ignoring the roil in my stomach whenever I think about what I was doing last summer compared to what I'm doing now.

I pass the vacant car lots with the sales event banners still taped to the windows, then the bread factory, where the grass is reclaiming the pavement. Just before the expressway I find Lafayette Estates—a trailer park that moonlights as a trash dump.

It's funny but not funny, our respective estates. Because I live at Fenwick Estates, a subdivision with three-car garages. It's all relative, I guess.

I've been to Lafayette Estates once or twice, but as I pull in the entrance, the car dips into a pothole with a scrape, and it's like a warning I've entered a warzone. I creep past the rows of crooked mailboxes, the tattered FOR RENT signs and FREE KITTENS flyers tagged to the posts, paint buckets, overturned couches, broken coffee tables, and too many splotchy mattresses to count. Then, around the turn, across from the rust-eaten trailer with the sun-bleached confederate flag hanging in the front window, I stop in front of Molly Martinez's trailer.

Two little girls play chase in the front yard. Molly stands guard on the porch, watching over them until she sees my car and bolts to attention. The taller of the two little girls stops and shields her eyes from the evening sun.

The sudden attention throws me off my game. I leave the car running, climb out, jamming my hands in my pockets as I try to come up with something to say. The younger girl hops in place, pointing at me. "Look, a giant."

"Look, a little person," I call back. The older girl giggles and runs up to me. She's wearing a light purple dress with grass stains around the hip. The little one catches up and peeks out from behind her with wide eyes and an adorable grin.

"Giant, giant."

Molly comes down the steps with a *what-do-you-want* stare in her eyes.

I look back to my car, then across the street to the confederate side, where it's all weeds and crabgrass. A couple of metal drums line the back part of the trailer where a dented air conditioner dangles from the side window. Ladders and buckets, a dented up truck sitting on cinder blocks, maybe its engine is the one dangling from a sagging swing set.

I suddenly feel the need to explain myself. "Hey, I was in the neighborhood."

It's a dumb joke, and an even dumber chuckle that comes with it. Behind Molly, the torn screen hangs from the door. Along the bottom of the trailer, litter is caught in the mud-stained lattice. The siding is broken and peeling off at the corner. Behind the sunflowers, the streaky windows are empty and dark. Next door sit three older-style sedans, all shiny with crazy paint jobs and big tires with rims. A faint thumping throbs from inside the trailer.

The whole place has me uneasy. Even as the little girls laugh and dance and call me giant. "Oh, um..." Molly turns and calls over to the girls. "Ash, can you and Ana go inside for a minute?"

The littlest drops her shoulders and pouts. "I don't want to."

I shake my head, wishing I hadn't come. Wishing a lot of things. "No, it's fine. I'll take off. I just...wanted to make sure everything was okay."

Molly folds her arms over her chest, gripping at her elbows, walking towards me but staring at her feet. "My mom had to work today. She took the phone." She sighs, blowing the hair from her face. "Can you tell Virgil I'll be in tomorrow, I mean, if..."

Some rumbling up the street. "No, yeah, he's fine. I spoke with him earlier."

Molly's eyes widen with what I mistake for gratitude until I realize she's looking past me, over my shoulder. I turn to find a primer-gray monster truck idling roughly behind my car, which reminds me I've left it running in the road.

"Hey, move your damn car."

The guy leans over a miserable looking woman to yell at me. Then he revs the engine, which roars then hiccups then nearly stalls. Across the windshield of the truck it reads, BAD HABIT in neon stickers. I start to laugh, which I realize is my own bad habit, before he revs the engine again. "Now."

I can't get a good look at the guy, but the woman's face is fried with wrinkles. She sucks on a cigarette so hard it looks like her cheeks are going to collapse.

Molly gathers the girls. She points to the door and orders them to get them moving. I run my hand through my hair, shoot her a look, then turn back to the guy in the truck.

"Um, yeah sure," I say to the redneck, only now noticing the rifle on the gun rack across the back window. I look back to Molly. "Well, see you tomorrow, right?"

She doesn't wave or seem to hear me at all. She stares down the guy in the truck as she backs the girls into the trailer. The lovely passenger hocks a lung and spits out the passenger window. I live in a subdivision where people are ticketed for not trimming the hedges. Can't say I'm used to this sort of thing.

"Okay, okay." I start around the car when the dude lays on the horn. I shake my head, trying to keep it together when he leans all the way out of his window. The brim of his hat is smeared with grease and has one of those hook things clipped to the visor. Judging from what I can see, he's a little guy with something to prove. "You got something to say?"

"Nope," I say, determined not to get into a fight every time I'm with Molly. But the guy can't drop it, he turns to the woman sitting in the middle, whose eyes scrape across my car like fingernails, like it's somehow to blame for all the crap that has ever happened to her—which, judging by her face is a lot. The driver points at me.

"Just as bad as these Mexicans."

I stop, fists clenching, a tight rage taking hold in my chest. I cock my head at him and he starts with the revving again. Only this time he puts the truck into gear. The engine sputters then catches and lurches ahead. I jump back as he misses my car by inches, swinging the truck over a rotted railroad tie and into the yard of the trailer across the street.

I stand at my car, dumbstruck, wondering what in the hell, when the guy leaps from his truck and makes a line for me. Fine, we can do this. I step forward, just as Molly's door slams shut and one of the girls starts crying. I stop myself and take a breath as this little redneck comes at me from the yard, jabbing a finger and muttering about gangbanger spics.

My car door is still open when he bends down and comes up with a rock about the size of a brick. He stops at the street, cocked. I put my arms up and start for my car, still determined to settle this rationally. "Look, I'm leaving. What's your problem, anyway?"

It's a big question. One that, from where I'm standing, would take a while to sufficiently address. The woman slides out of the truck and waddles over to the man. She's wearing one of those moo-moo things and glares at me. "We're sick of it," she says to me.

I get in the car and shut the door. I know I should leave, shouldn't even be here to begin with, especially when she flicks her cigarette and it lands in the road near my car. "Go somewhere else and get your drugs now."

"No, it's not—" I glance back to the trailer with the shiny cars. "No," I say, for some reason. "I work with Molly."

The lady is heaving for breath as she turns slowly and starts for her yard, hiking through the weeds and around the obstacles to the door framed with Christmas lights. I can only stare, thinking how at least one time they'd attempted to decorate. At least once they chose to try to be happy or celebrate something. Or maybe they didn't. Maybe it was left on the trailer when they moved in. She nudges the man back, and they start for the trailer, leaving me out there between those two hopeless rectangles. The man gives me a long, hard stare and reluctantly follows behind.

I let off the brake, slowly, smirking at the dude as I wipe back my hair. I glance over at Molly's trailer, hoping things are okay, when out of the corner of my eye I catch some movement to my left. Then something explodes in my car. More specifically, the glass just behind my head.

My foot mashes the gas to the floor. The tires spin and spit gravel before the car lunges forward and I bang into the first left and gun it. Mind racing, hands shaking, the last thing I see is that bald guy raging. He screams after me, arms out, daring me to come back.

He hurls a bottle next, but I'm gone, peeling out and flying out of the trailer park. The window is smashed, wind flying. I only turn to look back once I'm a few miles up the road. Then I'm eyeing the rearview, gasping for breath as my hands flop around on the steering wheel, mumbling about crazy rednecks. I keep turning back to the puddle of blue glass covering the backseat. The wind streams through the gaping hole in the back window. I run the next three red lights. Stop signs, too. I don't take my foot off the gas until I'm tucked away at Fenwick Estates.

In the driveway, I discover it wasn't a bullet that took out the window but a rock. More like a jagged ball of gravel and concrete. A trailer park meteorite.

Deep breaths. That just happened.

Now at home, far removed from Lafayette Estates, I'm pissed. I mean, yeah, I'm glad it was the window and not my head, but I want something to happen. He shouldn't get away with hurling rocks through people's windows. But I can't call the cops. I have a feeling things would be worse if I did.

And now I have my own problems. Because I only have collision insurance, so a rear window is going to cost me a paycheck. While the Honda used to be Mom's car, back when it was shiny and new and matched all the other shiny new cars in the neighborhood, now it's nearly twelve years old. Yeah, it's dented, unmaintained, and temperamental as hell, but it's mine. I'm the one who keeps it running. A good thing, too. There are way too many steep hills in Woodberry to bike.

By the time I get myself together and walk into the house, I'm still shaken and not prepared for problem number two: Mom, sprawled out on the floor, in tears, a ripped opened envelope at her side. Great, more mail.

"Where are we going to go, Nat?"

Just that quickly, the car window slides into second place on the worry list. Mom thrusts a fistful of papers at me. I recognize the letterhead from the city of Woodberry, and for a second I think it's the school board letter. Then I see the words *Delinquent. Foreclosure. Auction.* All sorts of reminders and threats. Basically, if we don't come up with some cash soon, we need to vacate the premises. I mean, I knew it was getting bad, it's all I can do to keep the lights on around here. I just didn't know it had gotten take-the-house bad.

I scratch the back of my head. I still have glass in my hair and now this is happening. I drop the notice, wondering if anything good will ever arrive in our mailbox again. "Did you call Herndon?"

Herndon is Dad's lawyer. *Was* Dad's lawyer, three years ago. He's not keen on taking calls from me or Mom, who sits up, knees beneath her, shoulders slumped, a mess of a woman in the middle of the floor.

Old Herndon would only lecture us about how Dan Reams let us have the house. That's how he put it to my mom one time: *He left you a house.* Only we can't afford to pay taxes on the house, much less maintain it. That's okay, good old Dan even left us some furnishings, the gracious prick. Let's see, there's one overstuffed leather couch, scratched and split in the lower corner, and two end tables, the surface of which hold an almost Olympic pattern of wineglass rings. On the mantel are a few pictures—mostly of me, one of Mom and me at the lake. Otherwise the room is a ramshackle of books, dishes, and remnants of my mother's crackpot projects.

Don't get married, ever, is what I've learned. Because once upon a time I opened Christmas presents in this same room. My dad watched with joy, or so I thought. But somewhere in the back of his mind, he was plotting his escape. It makes me think, back when Mom used to take my picture in here every year on the first day of school, was she only a hair strand away from losing it then? Because now we're doing this.

Her nose is leaking snot. It's gross. She swipes a hand over the horror show that is her face. "I left him three messages." She snatches the notice off the floor. "They can't do this, can they, Nat?"

I'm seventeen, and she needs my reassurance. Thoughts spin around in my head, my random Virgil quotable generator suggests, *Suck it up, kiddo.*

I'd like some reassuring, too. But that's going to have to wait. And I'd be interested in finding out if anyone else has ever tried to console their mom while Deee-Lite's *Groove is in the Heart* thumps throughout the living room.

"I don't know, Mom."

It's little help, but damn, I can't think. I can't do this right now. It hurts just to look at her. She used to have it all together. She was the one I looked to for comfort after a bad day at school. My mom used to take care of people. I saw it with my own eyes. She worked days/nights/swing shifts in the emergency room. She's seen all the awful things people can do to each other: gunshots, stab wounds, broken bones, overdoses, head trauma. I've been there plenty of times myself, visiting, watching her work, seeing her scoop up the chaos and trauma and knead it into something manageable. I've watched her comfort kids and adults, all hysterical and needing her guidance. Now she's drinking box wine from a pickle jar.

I lean down and give her a hug. "Look, I need to take a shower. Then maybe we can try to sort this out."

"Maybe you should call your father."

"What?" I freeze, wondering how she could drop this weight on my shoulders. How delusional is she, anyway? I haven't spoken to my dad in over a year, at least.

She wipes her nose again. "You can tell him to go suck a duck."

I turn away. "Right. That should do it."

In the shower, the hot water helps the muscles in my shoulders and neck uncoil. I rinse the grass and some wayward glass shrapnel off my back. As much as I like working outside, I love being clean after a long day of it.

What the hell happened at the trailer park? That woman, talking about gangbangers. Molly and those little girls. I can still hear the door slapping shut, her sister crying. I can't believe they have to live that way.

Not that I'm doing much better. Downstairs, Mom has re-upped on the wine and swapped out Deee-Lite for Cat Stevens. It kills me the way she chooses the most depressing songs when she's getting faced. It's hard to be around.

I check my phone. Three messages from Cora, my sort of ex-girlfriend. It's been a few days since a text or call. Our relationship is weird. We never broke up, technically, but I don't think Cora Conners is thrilled about dating a potential GED grad as opposed to an all-district basketball player. And I can't blame her for not wanting to hang, I'm not much fun to be around anymore.

She's casually retreating and I'm not sure I want to stop her. But downstairs, after being sure Mom is still sedated, swaying around, wailing along to *Morning Has Broken*, I step outside, back into the heat, and call Cora back.

She dives right in. "Um, hello? I've been trying to call you."

I resist the urge to tell her the world does not revolve around her calls. It might confuse her. "Yeah, been busy with work and all."

"Well, Jackson's parents are out of town. We're going over around eight. You want to pick me up, or—"

This is how it works with Cora. Days of avoiding my calls, but then I'm needed urgently. I take a breath. Maybe I called her because I'm stalling. Because Mom wants me to call Dad and I'm actually considering it. Been considering it, really. It's why I have his office number. I found it online.

"Cora, I can't. My mom's freaking out."

"Come on, Nat. Puhwheezie?"

Okay, so I'll admit it, the pouty voice used to work. Back when I was too distracted by Cora's, uh, assets, to pay much attention. And still, sometimes it's hard to just let it go. Like all the trophies in my room. Some in my closet. News clippings about how great I was. For three years you work and plan for your senior year. You see your name in the newspaper and you believe the hype. Yeah, sure, your mom is acting kind of crazy, but you're able hide it from everyone else and just play basketball and party. Then you end up in the wrong place at the wrong time and—*poof*— it's gone.

The person Cora knows so well was a different me. I can't deal with her right now. Besides, whatever you wanted to call our relationship has come and gone, and I've got way too much to worry about to be thinking of beach week and parties. And even if I wanted to do that stuff, I can't leave Mom alone.

But Cora Connors doesn't want to hear that. She's still where I was last year. It's kind of surprising she even called. But I can't do it, not after what just happened.

"Cora, listen—"

"Nat. It's summer. Stop being lame."

I don't need to see her to picture it. Tossing back her blonde hair, rolling those baby blues. Cora's short with curves in the right places. And it's almost enough to make me forget about Mom on the floor, cheeks shining, wet with tears; the car and the smashed-out window. It's tempting to leave, drive off and have some fun. But even then, it's not the same. All the stares I get. The whispers. It's like, once you punch a teacher, people form an opinion of you. Good or bad, it's not something you can shrug off.

Back in the house, Mom belts along to *Moonshadow* at the top of her lungs. I turn for the walkway, trying not to notice the high grass and weeds along the pavers. "Cora, really, I..."

I catch my breath, and before I tell her about the house, about how I don't know what Mom and I are going to do, even about the whole thing at Molly's place, someone giggles in the background. Loud voices on her end. Cora playing with someone else. It seems we've exceeded the bandwidth of our attention span. I doubt Cora, who cheated on me at least twice after I quit coming to school last year, will notice if I end the call. So I do.

Inside, I start for the jug of water when I spot a beer. I crack it open because, who cares? Back outside, I take down three deep swallows, nearly gag, and call the office.

I can call him, right? I mean after all, the guy *is* my dad. Then why am I sweating something crazy?

When my parents first split, I thought I'd have to decide where to live. I was thirteen and I'd watched too many sitcoms. I saw myself taking the stand, having to point to which parent I loved more. It stressed me out. But things never got so dramatic. There was no courtroom. Dad never invited me to live with him. He moved out and called every week at first, but then he didn't. I wonder what he'd think about me flunking out of high school.

I seriously doubt Dan Reams knows what kind of shape we're in. It hasn't been punched into a spreadsheet, the numbers haven't been crunched and analyzed. He's all about the profit margin. Where my dad is a walking PowerPoint presentation, my mom is a coloring book. It's surprising they ever got together in the first place.

Two rings. What am I doing? I haven't spoken to him in ages. What am I going to say? Doesn't matter, on the third ring the call goes to voicemail, like someone saw a call and pressed a button. I'm simultaneously relieved and disappointed.

This is Dan Reams. I can't take your call. If you need to make an appointment, please call during business hours. If you'd like to leave a message...

Beep.

All the things I could say to him hang on the line, hissing in my ear. I feel the sturdiness of his hands on my bike seat, I hear the confidence in his voice when I was too afraid to try. So many thoughts come and go and get like the haze of trimmings and dust when I'm cutting grass. About Dad and the good old days. His stubble on my face when he brought me in for a side hug. How he used to come to my games and pump his fist even while he had his work phone glued to his ear. But I can't dwell on that, there's no point. Because all I can do is record a message or call during business hours.

I sling the beer bottle at the car. It misses the gaping hole where the back window used to be and smacks the fender and shatters. The Honda is taking a beating today. And so am I.

I go inside, looking for another beer.

4

The next morning I'm jerked awake by a persistent banging at the front door. I sit up, head hurting, letting the debris of reality fall over me as I blink to consciousness. The morning sun is bright and urgent, a reminder that I'm going to be late once again.

The banging continues. But I'm not going near the door. I'm awake enough to recognize the knocking. There's a certain ownership to the raps, a crisp rhythm—no doorbell, just knuckles on wood. Sure enough, I peek out the window and find my favorite Army recruiter standing at attention, his hair buzzed painfully short so his skull glistens in the morning sunlight.

He consults his watch, rolling his neck like he's ready for a cage match. I check my phone, rub my head, and sigh. The guy could have at least called.

Another round of banging, more aggressively now. The recruiter takes a step back, like maybe the door opens drawbridge style. I'm content to let him have at it, it's not like he can wake Mom. Besides, it is sort of my fault he's here.

I've had lunch with him twice, soaking up his praises while throwing down some chicken chow mein and shrimp fried rice. The first lunch was low key, but something changed on that second date. He came on strong, sizing me up, making advances, talking ASVAB testing and physical requirements. Now he's making house calls.

There won't be a third date, that much is clear as he marches off, slamming the door of his government-issue Dodge Intrepid and peeling out of my life. It's bittersweet, because shrimp fried rice tastes better when it's free.

Once he's gone, I get moving. The car is a mess. Not just the smashed window or the beer bottle glass in the driveway but everything inside is slick with dew. I set the seat back and my hand sticks to the steering wheel. A wine bottle rests in the console. Looks like Mom had a good time last night.

I toss the bottle to the floorboard, almost hoping it breaks. I check the mirror, turn the key, and I'm throttled by a raspy blast of Janis Joplin. I smack buttons to stop the hemorrhaging. I'm not sure even Janis Joplin fans can handle Janis Joplin in the morning.

I'm backing out when Chase Andrews crosses the lawn and runs up to the car. He's the more likable of the twelve-year old twins next door, the only one who ever walks Pugsley, the Andrews' yapping menace. The brakes grind as I slow to a stop and give him a nod, because the kid's staring at me like I'm a maniac.

"What's up, Chase?"

Unlike his brother, Chase still thinks I'm someone worth impressing. He flings his blond bangs to the side. He's got a conspiratorial smile on his face. "Dude, what happened to your ride?"

I shrug, because I'm not in the mood.

"Are you joining the Army?"

"Huh? Oh, no." I look back up the road when it hits. Staff Sergeant, the guy's a Staff Sergeant. "Nope. Wrong house."

"He's been here before."

The kid takes after his dad, who happens to be the homeowner's association president. The Andrews don't miss a thing on our street. I've already gotten one notice about the clothesline, another about the broken shutter hanging off the upstairs window.

I let off the brake, the Honda makes a buzzing noise I haven't heard before. "Well, I'm late, gotta go."

Pugsley sends a few parting barks my way. Chase regards my ride with a fascinated grin, as though he's witnessing a real live steam engine in action. Then he's off for his house, crossing back to his green, freshly mowed lawn to spill the details to his brother, Chet, or worse, the president himself.

I find my boss sitting on the trailer, shaking his big head and making a show of his waiting. I swing the car in the lot and grab my things.

"Sorry Virgil, there was a wreck, traffic was—"

He holds up a giant hand. It's like a street sign, that paw of his. The trailer sighs with relief as Virgil slaps his legs and hoists himself up. "Well Nat's here, I guess we can get started."

Behind him, Molly Martinez is busy at work loading up the mowers, back to her role as perfect employee. "Sorry," I say to both her and Virgil, hopping up on the trailer to help. Virgil slurps his drink.

"You should get those brakes fixed. Heard you coming a mile away."

"Will do, Virg," I mumble. Because brakes, that's what I'm worried about.

Molly and I exchange glances. She looks the same. Same quiet stare, same head nod. Same t-shirt, sleeves rolled up revealing her toned, brown arms. She avoids my eyes, probably because she knows I have all kinds of questions about those people across the street. About her sisters. About her mom and about those guys next door. About her status. The list goes on.

She leaves with Virgil while I take the truck out to the bank. Later, when we get back, Virgil catches me in the garage. "So Molly says her mom had to work. She promised it won't happen again."

"That's cool." I make sure not to look at him. Virgil is the kind of guy who likes to lay down the rules, show he's in charge. I know he's only telling me this, even as he's wheezing something terrible, hoping I'll divulge any information I may or may not have.

Instead I make a graceful exit. I fill the gas cans with minimal spillage, straighten up, and find Molly sitting at the edge of the trailer.

"Hey, you need a ride?" I ask, my voice coming off a bit too hopeful.

She shakes her head. "No, I'm okay. Thanks."

I stand there for a second, kind of like Virgil did to me. I hate that I made things weird yesterday, coming to her house. When I take a seat beside her, she stiffens. Just when I thought things couldn't get weirder between us. "Look, I'm sorry I came by yesterday, okay? I just, I don't know... I just wanted to make sure."

She takes a deep breath, like she's about to say something, but doesn't. She looks past me, across the street. She looks at nothing. I lean in to get her attention. "So that dude..." Molly shakes her head, turns away, does anything but face me. I plow ahead. "Does that kind of stuff happen all the time?"

Her head drops. When she finally does look at me it's with complete exasperation. "Nat, what do you want from me?"

The plea in her voice, I've heard it once before. I shrug, because I really don't know what I want from Molly. But I've felt tied to her since last spring, like we've been chained to that day in the chem lab, the day our lives collided. The guilt and anger and...blame, I guess, I've carried ever since. I take a breath. "I want to help."

Her eyes flash hot, then it's gone. Blank, devoid of emotion. She gathers herself, grips the edge of the trailer as she gets to her feet. "You've helped me enough, okay? Just," her voice goes soft. "Just please don't do anything. I'll pay for the window, okay?"

There it is again. *Please don't.* But I can tell she's irritated with my prodding, which I continue. "Molly, I'm not going to *do* anything."

It's true. I haven't done much for myself, let alone my mom, or anyone else, really.

She waves it off and starts down the lot, walking towards the bus stop. Behind me Virgil coughs and hacks then spits. What *do* I want from her? Gratitude? Something else? I catch up to her. "Molly wait, just let me give you a ride."

She stops and turns, a bewildered smirk on her lips. She shakes her head and I'm surprised when she laughs. "Why would you want to come back? I mean..." She motions to my car, her eyes scanning the trash bag I've taped in place where the window used to be.

I laugh, nodding at my handiwork. "Looks nice, right?"

Molly remains unimpressed. But that almost smirk—she's got these dimples I've never really noticed because she never really smiles. She looks off again. "I think you should stick to Fenwick."

"Where's the fun in that?" I open the door. "How about a ride?"

She stares me down. Traffic shoots past. I keep a smile plastered on my face. Finally, she shrugs and huffs and walks past me and gets in the car.

We drive off, leaving work, the trash bag flapping in the wind. I'm content with her company. I don't try to talk her up. You can't out-quiet Molly Martinez. You can't out-sulk her, out-stare her, and you sure as hell can't out-think her. But this time it's different. Molly doesn't seem mousy but almost stubborn, determined, her arms crossed at her chest and her eyes like forged iron. But that's fine with me, because I've always liked a challenge. And I'm determined not to sit there and do nothing.

The idea hits as we approach her turn. It's crazy but then, so is my life these days. I work it out in my head until it almost seems doable. Probably because I usually agree with my own ideas until they blow up in my face.

Molly shifts as we pass the turn to Lafayette Estates. She looks back and then stares me down. If nothing else, the girl's fight-or-flight instincts are keen. "Where are we going?"

I shrug, now that she's in the car I keep thinking about her little sisters, the hopeless trailer, the redneck who smashed my window. "I was hoping we could talk."

Her eyes hit me like darts. "Are you kidnapping me? My mom works at six. I don't have much time."

I turn for River Ridge Park. "You know, I'll bet you're really funny when you want to be. Of course I'm not kidnapping you. I mean, is it okay? Can we go for a walk?"

She takes a breath, her eyes glancing over her shoulder, to the bag. "I'm kind of tired."

Fine. I park the car in full view of the basketball court. A game is going on, ten guys playing ball, dribbling, shooting, practicing, getting better than me at this very moment. I push away thoughts of my former life, everything but the steady hum of the radio. My thoughts are still zooming through my mind like passing trains, ideas fleeting, reality getting in the way of my blurry plan, messing things up. But still, after seeing Molly with her sisters, living where they do, I've got to do something.

I turn to Molly. "This is going to sound crazy."

Her eyes break away from the basketball game. She shifts in her seat for the hundredth time, raises an eyebrow. "Okay, that's one way to start a conversation."

The radio cuts to a commercial for new cars. "Come and get 'em!!!" calls the half-crazed voice. I hit the switch and it falls silent except for the faint yells and trash talking from the game on the court. Here goes nothing. "Molly, we have four bedrooms, five if you count the office my mom uses for storage. We have like, three full bathrooms, something like three thousand square feet of living space."

Shift. She crosses her arms and squints out the window. Because of our past, I've never exactly considered Molly as anything other than a victim. But her profile in the car, set against the light, reminds me of a painting. Even after eight hours of work, her hair shines, pulled tight into a ponytail, except for a few strands that fall down her cheek. Her eyelashes spill from her dark eyes, her skin is smooth and unblemished. And the dimples, along with the curve of her lips it's, well...

She gives me a look. "So you brought me here to brag about your house?"

I look away, regaining my thoughts. "No. I mean, we probably won't be there much longer, but..." I shake my head, trying to put the words in the right order. It sounded better in my head. Now, it's falling apart in spurts, half thoughts, half words. "Um, I don't know what's going to happen with everything, but, I mean..." A deep breath. "Why don't you—your mom and sisters I mean—you guys could stay with us for a while?"

Her head swivels. Her lips part. She cocks her head as her eyes widen then crease to a squint. A car drifts by, the bass so deep I can feel it in my seat. Molly exhales. "I'm sorry, *what?*"

I wipe my face, caught off guard by her expression, the strength in her voice, by what I'm doing. "No, um, I'm serious. Wouldn't it be safer, for your family?"

She's still squinting, slowly shaking her head like she's trying to figure me out. When she finally speaks, her voice is almost a whisper. "Why? Why are you—?"

Again, her mouth opens then shuts. She turns to her window but then whips back to me. "I mean, is this like something you want to put on a college application?"

I rub my forehead. "Molly, no."

She sits up straight, and suddenly she's bigger than I ever realized. Her gaze is focused now, and again I feel stupid for all the times I've misjudged her. She blows that loose strand of hair from her face. Her hands flap around her lap, clasping, unclasping. "Seriously, you punched the teacher forcing himself on the undocumented girl. Then you got her a job. Now, you want to take in her family, like a box of puppies."

I slam my head back into the seat. "Molly. Stop."

She slaps her palms on her legs, sets her face straight ahead, and closes her eyes. *Undocumented.* The word sits in the car like a passenger. I mean, I suspected, I guess. But to hear her say it out loud. She's undocumented. Okay, so it's settled.

The kids on the basketball court argue a call. I run a hand through my hair. It's getting long and starting to curl. "Yeah, Molly. You're right, this is all for my college application. Except, I'm probably not going to make it back to high school, so..."

She jolts forward, thumps a hand to her chest. "And that's my fault, right? Because I basically ruined your life." Her sharp, angry voice hangs in the silence that follows.

My phone dings but I don't even look. Molly turns to the window, says she needs to get back.

"Just think about it, okay?"

She stares out the window. Undocumented.

I start the car and we drive away.

5

I drop Molly off at her house. No one throws anything at my car. Her sisters aren't outside. I drive past the mattresses and litter boxes and pull out on the road, thinking about all the multiple exits to multiple streets, interstate highways, roads that lead out of here. All it takes is one exit, one turn, then just drive. Never look back.

Instead, I drive home without music or sound, only the flapping bag in the window. Gary's Volvo sits in the driveway. Again, I'm tempted to keep driving. I can't think of anything worse than walking in on my mom and old Gary, reading poetry, or...something gross. But mostly I'm still caught up in the conversation with Molly. Maybe I should at least run it by Mom that I've just invited a family of four to live with us.

I find her awake and peppy, sitting at the table in her pink nursing scrubs and a billowing green wrap around her head. Zippy Jazz music flows through the kitchen. Gary has stars in his eyes, as usual, and judging by Mom's mood, speech, and motor functions, she's about a third of a wine box in. Then again, it's kind of hard to tell anymore.

Gary stands as I enter, formal and stiff as he fiddles with a button on his blazer. Mom points at me and claps her hands. "Oh good. You're home. Now go shower and get dressed, we're going out to eat."

I'm in no mood to go anywhere with them, but I'm in no mood to cook, either. So I do as I'm told and take a quick shower.

Twenty minutes later, we step out of the house and into the still sweltering evening. Gary offers to drive, which is just as well considering my window situation. I'm only hoping old Gary doesn't try to talk me up too much. One time, when left alone, the guy went on for an hour about his trusty Yard Machine walk-behind mower. It was brutal.

Chase and Chet are out, chucking a football in the street. "What's up, Nat," Chet says with a smirk. "What happened to your ride, man?"

"It's a new feature. Side airbags."

Chet scoffs. Chase comes running up to me, his sweaty bangs plastered to one side of his forehead. He hands me the ball. "I'm going deep." Then he takes off running.

I grip the laces, measure his strides, cock the football back while Chet, the little rat, is backpedaling, prowling for the interception. I sling the ball over his outstretched arms, where Chase bobbles the catch but manages to bring it in for the score. I throw my hands up in victory. Chase does some sort of touchdown chicken dance.

"Nicely done," Gary says in his best Mr. Rogers impression. He gets the door for Mom, who holds her face up to catch the breeze, completely in her own world. As much as I hate on the guy, I have to admit, I never once saw my dad get the door for her.

I'm thinking it's going to be a long evening as Mom goes on about her latest submission, a short story titled, OUR ONE MOON. She's subbed it out to *Three Ponds Press,* and she's got her hopes up. The story is terrible, something about angels and homeless people, if I remember it correctly. Thankfully, I can hardly hear her over my growling stomach. I haven't eaten since lunch and it's going on six. At least the AC feels nice and the seats in the Volvo are cush.

Mom looks back, and I assure her the story is great. Call me lazy, but I can't imagine telling her it's anything other than fantastic. She thinks she's on the cusp—she can feel it. But with every rejection I watch her sink further beneath the covers, sleep later through the day. She may think she's some bohemian badass, but she's not, she's delicate; one tiny sliver of criticism and she's in her room for a week.

"Gary thinks I should play up the homeless angle," Mom says with a smile. Gary nearly goes careening into a ditch. I tune her out and let my eyes drift to the hedges around the houses, the thick green grass, the decorative crabapple trees waiting to be cut down and stumped, hauled off once they outgrow their purpose and become real trees. Then, before I can blink, it's back. Good times. High school, basketball, parties. How I fell into any distraction to get over the way Dad split, even when I secretly hoped it would pass over. Then afterwards, with the buzz and scholarship talk, how I thought Dad might give me a call. Never happened.

Even after the Meyers thing I was supposed to get up with DeShaun and play ball a few days a week this summer. Stay in shape and await my redemption. The plan, long ago, was DeShaun and I would play together at Woodberry College. Back when we led the high school team in scoring last year and made it to states. And while DeShaun has called a few times, I haven't heard a thing from Coach. Probably for the best, anyway. I find it's easier just not talking to anyone.

We pull into La Fiesta, the Mexican restaurant near Woodberry. It's busy, the wait staff flies past with sizzling plates, weaving around the people lined up to pay and the little kids trying to score candy or play video games up front. We take a seat on the bench and wait for a table. There's like ten TV's hanging on the wall, most of them showing a soccer match, but one is tuned to CNN, where the screen is split so two people can argue. Underneath it reads: CONGRESS/PRESIDENT STILL AT ODDS ON IMMIGRATION BILL.

Mom glares at the TV. Images of deportation centers and

desperate families behind fences. A senator from Texas talks about getting in line and doing things the right way. *Undocumented.*

I sink down in my seat because I already know what's about to happen. Mom is hard enough to manage at home, out in public things can get messy. I can usually tell when it's coming because she starts huffing and looking around. Outrage comes easy for Mom. Self-control, not so much.

She shakes her head. "This wall, for heaven's sake. It's a travesty. It's immoral!"

Gary and I exchange looks. I lean over and try to shush Mom as she tells anyone within earshot how the senator is a complete moron.

The TV flashes to a showdown at the border. A caravan of people lined up, being led into a bus. Immigration centers with people sprawled on the floor, ICE agents, military figures who remind me of my favorite Army recruiter. It all gets me thinking. I'm not cut out for military, combat, removing people. I was only looking for a way out of my own mess.

The images on the screen only get Mom more worked up. "We're all immigrants!"

"Yeah, okay, Mom."

People at the register are side-eyeing us. A guy with a gut that could fill a lawn bag turns and glares at her. My thoughts are all over the place—the conversation with Molly, her family, how I couldn't give her an answer as to why I want to help. At the same time people are watching Mom, who sighs dramatically, clicks her teeth, and smacks her leg and basically dares anyone to debate her on this.

Gary's torn between comforting my mom and getting her to shut the hell up. I wonder if he's ever given much thought to how much work it would be to actually "court" my mother, to use one of his phrases. He has no idea.

Thankfully, we're seated before Mom can incite a riot. And as we get a table and Gary pulls out the chair for Mom, I'm thinking it's as good a time as any to let her in on what I have planned—which technically boils down to harboring undocumented immigrants.

Pretty sure it's illegal, but looking at this woman sitting across from me, the explosion of color, publicly putting elected officials on blast, I can't imagine she would object.

Gary carefully unfolds his napkin and places it on his lap, takes a quick peek around as Mom fumbles through some cringe-worthy Spanish with the waiter. She orders two *cerveza's*. She and Gary discuss vegetarian options. A clasp of her hands and her eyes light up. "Oh, so tomorrow night, the writer's group is meeting at the house."

"Oh, that's cool," I say, casually as ever. Then, in the Mexican restaurant, where she's butchering the Spanish language and making a fuss over immigration laws, assuming everyone agrees with her, I figure now's a good a time to put her morals to the test.

I grab a chip, smirk at Gary, then turn to my mom. "Hey Mom, that reminds me, I need to ask you about something."

6

It's crazy what miles of push mowing in the heat can do to reality. Where I'm the star of my daydreams, ripping off my warm-ups and running layup drills, a sea of Woodberry maroon and silver in the stands as I crack the starting lineup, maybe even making all-conference a few years down the road. I'm the talk of the town, making the evening news, wiping my forehead while stressing the results of hard work and discipline.

The next minute I'm on CNN, praised as a hero for my actions against an abusive teacher. Me, in a crisp polo. I've finally gotten a haircut, the scroll below reads, *Student saves quiet, unthankful classmate from aggressive teacher*. Or something like that. And there's Mom, at La Fiesta, sucking down margarita's and telling anyone who will listen about her brave son.

I'm off in this unhealthy sort of glory when I hit a stump with the mower and get jolted back into the haze of reality.

Fact check: I'm currently expelled. Expelled basketball players do not get scholarships to college. My school board meeting is weeks away. CNN never called. The mower needs gas.

I have no idea what to expect at the school board thing. Ideally, I would explain why I decked Mr. Meyers and the powers-that-be would believe me and he'd get what he deserved. Again with the glory. Look where that got me.

We break for lunch and I hustle to the car. I hit up East Ridge, where all the convenience stores and fast food places line both sides. I get lucky with the traffic lights and make it back in ten minutes with Subway. I find Molly under an oak tree and offer a double chocolate cookie, her favorite.

"Thanks," she says quietly.

I sit down, unwrap my meatball sub, tear into a bite and start talking through a mouthful of food. "So, I spoke with my mom. She's cool with the arrangement. Actually, she thinks it's a great idea."

True story. At the restaurant Mom had leaped from her seat, scattering chips and nearly knocking over her *cerveza*. She'd hugged me, nearly in tears, while Gary sat motionless, looking awfully skittish about what I was proposing. I could tell he was distancing himself from any possible legal implications, especially when Mom spent the rest of the weekend painting, or, nesting—as she'd called it —nearly euphoric over the prospect of Molly's two little sisters scampering around the house.

I don't tell Molly any of this. I stick to the facts as she sits back, knees pulled to her chest and her head against the tree, unusually pensive, even for her.

I do what I always do around Molly: keep talking. "I mean, you guys would have to put up with a lot. She stays up late, throws wild writer parties because she thinks she's Jane Austen or something. She's highly delusional, she'll talk your ear off about anything. Otherwise, she's harmless."

I shrug, take another bite, chew, wipe my chin. "So, I mean, if you guys get tired of living across the street from a lunatic, then, well... there's two bedrooms downstairs, a bathroom between them. However you want to work it out with the little people."

Molly closes her eyes, a small crease of dimple forming as I finish the first half of my sub and start in on the other.

"I love this campus," she says, as a slight breeze finds us. I look around, then back to her. I'm not sure if she's heard anything I said. Why do I care so much? But she's right, the Woodberry campus is a nice place to dream.

"Me too," I say, finally, and we gaze out at the grounds. The wrought iron, the ivy, the stone buildings. We breathe in the fresh cut grass, mulch, a tinge of exhaust in the air. We soak it all in.

I'm thinking about opportunities and consequences when Molly takes a deep breath, turns her head to me, and starts talking.

"In the fifth grade, we were studying the founding fathers. Mrs. Turner announced we'd be going on a field trip to see all the monuments in Washington, D.C."

A group of students saunter across the grounds, all smiles and book bags. Maybe freshmen arriving early, maybe orientation. Our mowers sit ticking and hissing nearby, separating us from them—the help from the students. Molly doesn't seem to notice. Or care.

She blinks, sets her gaze back out to the grounds, lost in thought. "I was *so* excited. I ran home, pounded on the door until Mom let me inside, and I told her all about it. I was going over the schedule, the stops and places, the dates. Oh, and I needed my social security number. Soon as I said it her face went cold. She was pregnant with Ash and my dad was out of town working. I asked if she was okay, if she needed anything. She told me to sit down."

She's not crying but her jaw is set to keep her lip from trembling. She looks down, then forces her chin back up, to the sun. "She told me I didn't have a social security number. That I wouldn't be going on a field trip. It was better I knew now. I was lucky to be in school. Sorry baby, this is how it is and there is no way to change it."

It's nearly ninety degrees out and I'm covered in goosebumps. Molly hugs her legs tighter, her hair falling to her arms. I loved field trips. Laughing on the bus, cutting up, the teachers yelling back for us to be quiet. You couldn't tell us anything back then. Another round of laughter comes from the students on the grounds. That was us.

She bites her lip, nods. "I'm kind of limited when it comes to choices, Nat. I didn't know those limits when I was little, I thought I was like my classmates. We'd been in school together since I could remember. I learned about limitations like history or math. I learned I couldn't do certain things." She throws her hands towards the students. "I'm still learning, like how I have no way to go to college."

"Molly. You're like the smartest person in school."

"We're getting evicted." She ducks her head, hiding her eyes. Her voice cracks. "My mom says we can pay you."

It's crazy, while Mom was celebrating, Molly was having a different sort of conversation. I slide closer to her. Like me, Molly daydreams, too. She dreams of going to college. Only there are no adoring fans, just some far-off hope of legitimacy.

I reach for her hand. "Molly, no, that's...no. It's fine. You guys can come tonight, okay?"

She nods, then looks up and stiffens. Virgil approaches. He stops, seeing us. Molly wipes her face.

Our afternoon is pretty chill, I figure why not get a start on the move? "Hey Virg, we're going to need to cut out early, okay?"

He does the big breath sigh. He's dripping with sweat even though Molly and I have done all the push mowing. "What? Both of you?"

I nod. He eyes us over, then cocks his head at me, and I know what he's thinking.

"What's going on?" he says,

"I need to help Molly with some personal business."

He looks us over, shakes his head. "Knew this would happen."

Oh no. Molly and I scoot away from each other. "No, Virgil, it's..."

Molly makes another swipe at her eyes before she looks at him, clears her throat. "I'm really sorry about the time off recently."

Virg looks off, kicks at the dirt. "It's okay, I guess, just, I'm going to need you to be in early tomorrow. We've got that place over at Crestview."

We both nod as Virgil stomps off and starts loading up. We

scramble to our feet to help him, moving mowers and weed whackers, making noise and doing anything besides looking at each other.

Back at Lafayette Estates I'm relieved to find my favorite redneck's truck is not in the yard. My relief vanishes when I see Molly's other neighbors sitting on the porch, watching, one guy on a weight bench in the yard.

Molly rubs her hands on her pants. She turns to me. "Um, could you, maybe, stay out here?"

"Oh, yeah sure."

She closes her eyes, takes a deep breath like she's trying to mentally prepare herself. "Thanks, I'll go check on the girls."

She starts to gather her bag and thermos.

"Shouldn't you just, I mean, leave it?"

She stops, face flushed. "Oh, right."

I check the rearview as Molly ducks out of the car and hurries to the trailer. The door slaps shut, and then it's just me and those four guys sipping beer and staring. I'm fiddling with the radio when it occurs to me I should probably clean the car out some. I've gotten most of the glass out of the backseat but there's still some on the floorboards. I start wiping down the backseat, willing myself not to think too much about what I'm doing or what might happen, moving stuff around in my trunk, when I hear giggling. "Look, it's the giant."

Molly's sisters rush out and latch onto my legs like we're best friends. Molly follows with two pillowcases stuffed full, spilling with clothes. She sets them in the yard and darts back inside, and then she's back with boxes, toiletries—a few tampons spill out and I pretend not to notice. I pick up little Ana and twirl her around.

"Attack of the giant," I roar, trying to make a weird situation normal. "Attack!"

Ana squeals and kicks her feet. I set her down, and she scampers off, giggling, as I chase her and Ashley around the small yard. They run circles around me and I'm thinking how great it is for little kids because this would be so much worse and depressing without them. Even when I hear the laughing and snickering next door. Even when Ashley says, "Are we coming to live at your house?"

I nod as the door squeaks open. Molly bulls through with more boxes. I try to help, more nodding and smiling at her mother who's speaking in Spanish. Molly rolls her eyes, replies in Spanish, then storms past me. Her mother goes back inside. The door smacks shut and it hits me with just how much my life has changed. A year ago I was playing AAU ball, thinking about the beach, Cora, partying, and junior year. Now, I'm watching Molly and her mother argue with an almost identical fatigue on their faces.

I hold the door as Molly's mother struggles with large canvases under both arms. Again, I hurry over, offering to help, ignoring Molly's annoyed sighs somewhere behind me. I take an armful from her mother, catching a glimpse of the top canvas. A street scene, a bluish green sky, people having dinner along a terrace on the boardwalk, a small brass band, seagulls skimming over the water. I can basically hear the waves crashing.

"Wow."

Molly's mother smiles and nods graciously. I'm about to ask if she's an artist when Molly snatches it from my hands and storms back down the stairs for the car. She shoves the canvas in my trunk like she's hoping to tear it. Her mother shakes her head, helplessly. I'm about to ask what's going on between them when Molly's mother launches into me with a powerful embrace.

I look at Molly, her own portrait of discomfort. "Mom says thanks."

"Yeah, no problem," I nod, my voice catching. Molly stares at her feet.

We fill the car with their lives—boxes of clothes, bags, books, and a few picture albums—and even though I tell Molly it's no trouble to come back, everyone seems content to leave it behind like the place is on fire.

Molly's eyes keep darting to the trailer next door where the sound of the metal bar clangs on the rack, then across the street. She's got a hardened look in her eyes, as though she's ready for battle. I get the girls seated amongst the boxes, but when Molly offers to squeeze in with them, her mother insists, clutching Ana in her arms. I drive as carefully as I've ever driven in my life, the girls asking a gazillion questions about the bag in the window. Molly shushes them, tells them to mind their business.

I make up silly jokes. I tell them the window shattered because I sneezed too hard. They get a kick out of that, cackling while Molly shakes her head, wiping her hair from her face, trying to hide a smile.

At the traffic lights the stares come. The bag, the boxes, my seat pushed to the dash so my face is almost against the windshield. The bag in the window flutters. We're all quiet as we get up the road, wondering how this is going to work out, when I say quietly to Molly, "Did you warn your mom about my mom?"

She shakes her head. "Stop. She can't be that bad."

I look straight ahead. "Okay. We'll see."

7

———

My mom has spent the day cleaning the house. In other words, drinking wine, cranking Joss Stone, and wearing a bandanna around her head while dragging furniture from one end of the house to the other.

She greets us in the doorway, flushed and out of breath. "Well hello-a-*hola!*"

I sigh at her makeshift Spanish. She's a box of wine in, easy. I watch Molly take her in, from her plaid Toms to the nursing scrubs and rubber gloves to the yellow bandana. Mom peels off the gloves and takes Molly's mom by the hands.

"*Gracias,*" Molly's mom says, nodding.

My mom smiles like a loon. "*Gracias* as well."

Whatever that means. I step forward. "Um, Mom, this is Molly Martinez, her mother. And these two little people here are actually fairies who have arrived to drag me back to their kingdom."

Ana and Ash giggle. Mom bends down, almost gracefully, until she steps back to catch her balance. "Oh my goodness. Aren't you two adorable?"

The girls look sheepish. Mom stands up straight and smiles as she takes in Molly. "And you are just, just…"

To my mom, everything is over the top. Beautiful. Fascinating. Adorable. Jet rocket highs and subterranean lows. But I really need to put a stop to this. "Mom."

She raises her hand. "Hush, Nat. You didn't tell me she was gorgeous."

I've never seen Molly blush before, and I'm kind of getting a kick out of it. But still. "Mom."

"Okay, okay, sheesh." She slaps my chest. "Get their things," she commands. Then, to our guests, her voice is soft and pleasant, "I'll show you to your rooms." My mom, the world's most dramatic concierge.

I start for the door as Mom gives the tour. They're about the same age, our moms, same height, but that's where it ends. It's easy to see they come from two very different planets.

Molly's mom looks around as though our house is the Smithsonian. The girls' laughter bounces off the walls. And while I can only imagine what her mom is thinking, I have a pretty good idea what is going through Molly's head as she hangs back, quiet, taking in the pictures in the hallway. This is killing her.

I haul in the bags of clothes, the boxes, the books and toys. I set the paintings carefully against the wall. When I return, Molly is still in the living room. I shrug, looking around, still feeling the urge to explain myself. "So yeah, I'm not doing this to be noble. I'm doing it because," I nod towards the steps. "I mean, look what I have to live with. I need some help."

Molly rolls her eyes. "Your mom is cute. I like her."

"Cute. Yeah, she's *real* cute."

To my surprise, Molly smiles. "Be nice."

"Okay, but I warned you."

Molly insists on rooming with her sisters so their mom can have her own bedroom. Mom claims there's a single bed in the attic. But for now, there's one queen-sized bed for the three girls.

I stay busy in the kitchen, where I'm surprised by the pool of warmth that finds my chest at hearing voices in the house. It's kind of comforting to have other people around. And it does feel like we're doing something good. Still, I keep hearing her voice, when she asked me why I'm doing this.

I can't put it into words. Ever since I saw Mr. Meyers grabbing at Molly, pulling on her, I've wanted to do something. I mean, something other than mash him in the face.

Once we're settled, Mom comes flying into the kitchen. She's mission-walking, what I call it when she marches off, mumbling some ridiculous notion in her head. She pours a glass of wine then starts flinging open cabinets. "I should cook us a dinner. A celebratory dinner."

"We have ramen," I say, looking over the scattered mail on the table, now burying the school board letter.

Mom whirls around, her eyes wide and wild. "No, no, Nat. We have guests at the house. We need *food*."

"What do you have in mind?" I'm somewhere between baffled and irritated at how matter-of-factly she's acting. "I've got," I lean forward and reach for my wallet, "eighteen bucks. Oh, and I need to put gas in the car."

Mom doesn't hear me because she's off in Mom-Land, slamming cabinets and searching for ingredients that only exist in her head. It's as though she's been away on a trip the last few months and has only just now discovered our current lot in life. "Hmm," she says. "I'm thinking linguine. With cauliflower and brown butter."

"Delightful," I say, humoring her. "Sounds incredible, really. So the ramen is up one shelf. To your left."

"I'll need sage, fresh parsley, maybe pine nuts and..."

Even with Molly and her family here—maybe *because* they're here—it makes me itchy hearing it. Where there was warmth and comfort, now anger sparks up my spine and settles in the back of my head. A flash of heat in my voice. "Mom."

She spins around towards me. "Yes, dear."

A quick glance around and I pull it together. I blink twice, lower my head. "We don't have any money."

"Nonsense," she says. "Let me find my purse."

I watch in disbelief as my mom marches out of the room, only to return digging into what looks like a burlap sack. Keys and change jingle as she finds her wallet. She fingers through it, picks out a card, and hands it to me without looking.

A quick recap here. I've taken showers with dish soap. I've called the electric company too many times to count in the past year, sitting on hold for nearly an hour so I could set up a budget plan and pay whatever minimum payment so not to have the power shut off. And I'll say this, those fast food napkins have not done my ass any favors. Now she hands me a card, for freaking linguini.

"What is this?" I ask, my jaw tightening at the sight of a Visa card from some sort of credit union.

She waves me off. "Take Molly with you," she says with a wink. "She's cute."

8

I snatch the credit card and stomp out into the evening. Molly tags along, both of us still wearing our matching lawn care shirts, smelling of cut grass, both of us still trying to make sense of what's going on. And it's while I'm not-so-secretly raging that Mr. Andrews comes bouncing down the steps of his house towards the car in his driveway.

Just great.

"Nat," he says, ducking into the backseat for his sport coat. I mumble a quick hello without stopping.

Mr. Andrews is a buff dude for a guy around forty. He goes to the Y every morning and likes to tote around his gym bag like a tool. He loves to let me know about what golf course he's played or what he's benching, following it up with, "Not bad for a guy in his forties." It's annoying. Back when Dad first split, he'd stop by and chat me up whenever he saw me in the yard, maybe trying to have a man-to-man. But I didn't want that with Mr. Andrews. Not then, not now. I want him to leave us alone.

"Ouch, what happened there, bud?" he says, nodding towards the

Honda, fiddling with his cuffs. His eyes find Molly and stick for a blink before he whips on the coat and shuts the door. He steals a peek at himself in his own window. "Did someone break in?" he asks, stretching into the sleeves, sucking at his teeth, pretending to be uninterested. Doesn't have me fooled, though. I know he's ready to file a report.

I shrug. "Nope. Kicked up a rock with the mower."

He nods, eyes back to Molly. "Oh, well, you guys staying busy?"

I can't do this right now. I nod, open the car door. "Yep, you know. Grass keeps growing."

He's waiting for me to introduce Molly. I'm not going to do it. Another click of the teeth before he looks over his own, lush lawn. "You know, if I could get the boys to do some work around here, it would save me a ton. But they've got soccer camp. A-League, stuff, this year."

I've learned not to engage Mr. Andrews when it comes to Chase and Chet. They're decent athletes, but to hear him say it, they're prodigies or something. He's got them in all sorts of clubs: lacrosse, soccer, golf, when all they want to do is play football and basketball. "Cool, well," I make a move with the keys. "We've got to go."

Mr. Andrews consults his Apple watch. Like my dad was, he's all business all the time. The kind of guy who can't take a simple walk without some sort of metrics. Always on the go, always knowing exactly what my dad will or won't be happy about.

"Right," he says, without looking up. "Take care, Nat. Oh, wait. Did you get the notices about the clothesline?"

All that small talk just so he can get to the point. I smile. "Sure did."

He nods twice, waiting for me to go on. Instead I keep smiling. Still smiling as Molly and I get in the car and I turn the key and we back out of the driveway.

I grip the wheel until it hurts. Because, a clothesline, he's worked up about a *clothesline*. Suddenly, I'm overwhelmed with how stained and battered my car looks. How it idles rough and it needs brakes and an oil change. How Mom has a magic credit card. How she's allowed to be hopeful and delusional while I have to go cut grass day after day with nothing, absolutely nothing, to look forward to anymore.

"Nat?"

"Huh?"

Molly's eyes are full and soft, reading into my thoughts. I wipe my face and smile, put the car in drive. "Sorry, I just…"

She nods, gives me a small smile but doesn't ask a bunch of questions. I nod and shake it off and we get down the road.

Molly stares at the houses, the green lawns, the wide driveways leading up to monster garages. She turns and looks at me. "So you don't get along with your neighbors either, huh?"

It makes me laugh. I think about her neighbors compared to mine. Here, at Fenwick at least, the battles aren't in the streets, but they're every bit as aggressive. Calls to the HOA. Notices about grass lengths and shutter colors. I drum on the steering wheel. "That guy, he's a first-class asshole."

She smiles.

I shrug. "What?"

A big dimply grin. "You're not allowed to have a clothesline?"

"Nope." I don't tell her how we'll probably get more HOA notices about our new living arrangement. She's a smart girl, but I'm not sure I can adequately explain to her my neighborhood dynamics.

She turns and gazes out the window again. I want to tell her she's safe now. But honestly, my neighbors aren't much better than hers. While Mr. Andrews would never hang a Confederate flag in his window (it is, after all, a violation of policy), how will he feel about living next to undocumented citizens? And what does that even mean, anyway?

It's been a day. I put my window down and fiddle with the CD player. Al Green's *Love and Happiness* thumps through the speakers. I hit the gas. Molly's hair catches the breeze. Over the wind and the music and the bag flapping in the window, it's hard to tell if I'm talking out loud or simply thinking in my head.

"There we go. That's better."

WE GET BACK AROUND FIVE. I take a shower and force myself not to think about neighbors, property taxes, board meetings, or anything else on my worry list. I find gym shorts, yank a t-shirt over my head, and shuffle down the stairs. Then I stop, because it feels like I've been hit with pepper spray.

Roughly two seconds later a smoke alarm starts chirping.

I come bounding around the stairs and leap over the railing. Little girl screams join the screeching alarm in the kitchen. By the time I cross the living room, I'm covering my face with my shirt to cover the sharp smells leaking from the kitchen.

"Mom, what are you doing?" The kitchen is thick with smoke. I rush in, directly into a downpour of water. At first I think it's some type of sprinkler system I'd never noticed. But no, it's Mom, drenching the stove with the sink sprayer.

I wave my hands in the air, fighting through the storm of smoke and water. The shriek of the alarm and the screams only add to the chaos. I get to the sink and shut the water off just as Mom appears with a box of baking soda and slings that into the mix. "I was just, I was boiling the..." She drops the box. She's heaving and wild. I step on a loaf of wet bread. Behind me come rushing footsteps, frantic Spanish. Molly's mom ducks in, takes my mom by the arms.

I jerk the window open, still crunching and smushing things on the floor. As things begin to clear, the damage is evident. The filthy dishes and baking powder all over the counters serve as a glaring reminder of my mom's failures at doing the most basic tasks. I yell over my shoulder. "What the hell, Mom? I mean, what are you cooking, I mean, besides pepper?"

A slap on my arm. I turn to find Molly, shaking her head and telling me to "be nice" between coughs. Meanwhile the girls watch closely from the other room, taking in my mom, the crazy lady who can't cook.

Be nice. I take a breath to calm down, tucking my nose in my shirt.

I flip on the ceiling fan and fling open more windows. When the smoke clears, quite literally, it's clear Mom has set fire to the box of linguini. A jar of some sort of sticky goo is smeared over the counter and the "steamed" vegetables are charred black. In the other room, Molly's mother sits with mine on the couch, stroking her head like she's a victim of some natural disaster. It's too much. I roll my eyes.

The smoke alarm keeps pounding away, blasting my eardrums. Everything is trashed. Anger at Mom swells inside of me for being like this, especially tonight. I reach up and rip the alarm off the ceiling, about to hurl it against the wall and start raging when I find Molly, lips parted, watching me.

I catch myself with a breath and a laugh that doesn't sound like my own as I make a show of gently popping the back of the alarm off and picking out the battery. I shoot her a smile. "Again. Welcome to my house."

Molly drops her shoulders. She leans against the doorjamb and shakes her head with a laugh.

We gather the girls and herd them outside for fresh air, to the overgrown backyard, riddled with weeds and ticks, towards my old, splintered jungle gym.

Ashley runs for the swings. Ana starts up the slide, slips, and shoots to the bottom. "Be careful!" Molly calls out and I laugh. I'm still sweating, a horrible after-shower sweat. My shirt smells like pepper and my chest is tight and it's all I can do not to scream. But if Molly hadn't been in the kitchen earlier, I would have screamed. I would have broken things. Things might have gone from bad to worse.

Now outside, it feels like I can breathe. I look at Molly. "So, yeah, this is what I was talking about. And you thought I was kidding,"

"I'm sorry," Molly says suddenly, still watching the girls.

"What?"

She shakes it off. "No, about...everything. I should be more grateful." She toes at something in the grass. "My mom tells me that all the time."

I wonder how Molly could possibly be more grateful. The girl who couldn't even go on a field trip. Couldn't go to school admins, or even authorities, after what happened at school for fear of being deported.

Deported. The word conjures up caravans on the news, people leaping over fences at night. Not Molly, who is every bit as American as I am. More, really. Most people I know wouldn't have cared one way or another about a trip to D.C. to see some old monuments.

I glance back at the house, where the kitchen windows are open to clear out the smoke. "Does your mom speak any English at all?"

Molly turns to me and blinks. "Some. I've been trying to help her but between work and," she nods at the girls, "she's usually too tired to study."

"Yeah, I get that." I wipe my forehead. "Well, as you can see, my mom doesn't speak much English either."

She smiles, tossing her black hair back over her shoulders. She's changed clothes too, now in a t-shirt and khaki shorts. Her legs are nicked up below the knees—what happens when you weed-whack in shorts. "I think you're too hard on her."

"Yeah, how was your dinner tonight? Mine sure was spicy."

"Guys, watch!" Ana calls out from the top of the slide. She inches down the four-foot slide and plops on the lawn.

"Amazing!" I applaud. Ashley furrows her brow and gives her sister an *I-can-do-better* look of disapproval.

Ana gets to her feet triumphantly, her eyes wide and proud. "Want me to do it again?"

Molly sighs. "Be careful."

I nudge her and call out. "Again, again."

Ana starts for the slide. Molly smiles at me. "Obviously you're going to be a bad influence."

Walking backwards for the swings, I smirk, holding out my arms, but my head catches the notorious clothesline. "Ouch."

Molly covers her mouth, trying to stifle a giggle. I turn for the girls. "Okay, who wants a push?"

Both girls raise their hands. I turn back to Molly with a smirk. "Obviously I'm the fun one."

9

At four minutes after eight on Saturday morning I'm jostled out of bed by the sound of a mower. It wouldn't be the first time I've dreamed about mowing grass. Endless strips of green, hills and hills to push mow, grass sprouting tall and thick so it's like a forest just as soon as I turn to make another swipe. Only this is not a dream.

It's Molly, cutting the lawn.

I snatch some clothes off the floor. My Larry Johnson Charlotte Hornets jersey, jogging pants. I'm mumbling to myself as I hit the steps. "It's our freaking day off."

A mechanical groan comes from the kitchen. I kick an empty wine box and it goes skidding across the floor. Wads of paper towels lay behind the couch, and a row of jars and glasses on the mantel make up her fly farm. I turn off the lamp, its glow useless against the morning sun. On the side table is a legal pad, some adult coloring books, and a mound of spent tissues, soaked to a ball from her tears.

Then I enter the kitchen.

Shining counters. Clean, empty sink. The mail is neatly stacked, and all the empty water bottles, socks, magazines, and Fig Newton wrappers are gone. The peppery gunk from last night's cooking fiasco has been scrubbed, and someone's taken out the trash. The burnt smell is replaced by a faint lemony scent. I realize the groaning noise is the sound the dishwasher makes when it's in use. Huh.

It looks like old times. Clean the way Dad liked it. I remember some epic fights in this kitchen. When I was in middle school Mom was just starting to show a glitch in the system. Little stuff, like walking home from the grocery store because she didn't feel like driving. Or when she quit using laundry detergent because of chemicals. How she liked to climb out on the roof at night and study the stars. I joined her a few times, trying to tap a telescope into her head, to understand what she was seeing, what was happening to her.

Anyway, one night, I was maybe eleven, Mom and Dad came home from some company party with Dad and the office guys. Dad was furious with Mom about getting drunk and, as he put it, "making an ass out of yourself."

It seems like nothing now, but back then it was like the world was coming to an end. I was standing in the doorway with the babysitter, watching my parents, all dressed up and sloppy drunk, cursing at each other. I think it was the first time I'd seen my mom like that, swaying on her feet, her eyelids heavy and her glass of wine spilling as she nearly tipped over. I remember at the time thinking, what happened to my beautiful mom?

Dad wasn't doing any better, flushed and sweating with too much white in his eyes. He looked like a troll, thrashing all over the place, livid about Mom dancing with some guy. They went on for ten or twenty minutes before either of them saw me or the babysitter watching them. Twenty minutes, but something changed between my dad and I forever. I could never look at him without thinking about that night.

I shake off the memory and find the school board letter. I stick it on the fridge, in plain sight, then snatch a water. A quick glance out back. Yeah, Molly, out there on the clock, her diagonal mowing pattern shimmering in the freshly trimmed grass. I'm about to run out and stop her, but why? She wants to help. Her arms, dark from the days in the sun, flex with movement. Her hair is set up in a loose bun instead of the usual ponytail she wears at work. Her face is tight with concentration. I can't help wondering what's going on in her head.

I'm still standing there watching when I hear something behind me.

I turn to find Molly's mom. She peeks up at me with a shy smile. I don't know how long she's been watching me watch Molly. I feel my face flush hot. "Oh, good morning." I clear my throat. "Um, did you... did you clean all this?" I motion to the counters.

She nods, her gaze scanning the floor.

It looks amazing. "Thank you so much. And thanks for taking care of my mom last night."

"She's...nice?"

I nod. "Um, yeah."

I wolf down a bowl of Fruit Loops while Molly takes on the backyard. By the time she starts fiddling with the trimmer, it's all I can take. I storm out and motion for her to hand it over. "You know it's Saturday, right?"

She shrugs. I shake my head. Molly hangs around while I trim and soon we're doing what we do: raking and weeding. We tackle the flower beds then shore up the crepe myrtles. The sun climbs and it gets hot. But even though it's Saturday it feels good to fix up the yard, to work at our own pace.

We don't say much as we tidy up the potted plants, edge the patio. We wash the sludge off the back windows and work our way along the side yard to the front, cleaning up the pavers and ripping out weeds.

I get into it, the sun and the dirt and it doesn't even feel like work. I find some tools and tighten up the bolts of the swing set. I'm yanking out a vine from the boxwoods around the side when Cora walks up on me.

"Hey there. I heard some laughing and so I came around."

"Oh." I wipe my face. Molly, on the other side, stands and

squints, then makes a move for the patio. Cora watches closely then sort of hisses at me. "What is *she* doing here?"

"Who? Molly? Oh, she's helping me in the yard."

Cora tosses her blonde hair back and I catch a familiar scent. I realize how ridiculous my response sounds. Molly retreats inside. Cora's eyes flash. "She just walks into your house like that?"

"So, what's up?" I say, trying to force some normality into the conversation. Cora shakes her head, checking her phone, then eyes the back door again. I pick at a thorn lodged in the skin between my thumb and index finger. I'm thinking it's way too early for Cora to be here, until I realize it's nearly lunchtime.

"Well, I wanted to see if you were coming out to Jackson's tonight. Or ever, really."

Jackson's parents go out of town approximately every four days, so his lake house is the spot to crash. It used to be fun, but now, I can't imagine hanging out with the old crowd. I wipe my brow. "I don't know. Mom's having one of her writer get-togethers, I better stick around and make sure nothing gets out of hand."

She rolls her eyes. "Yeah, *that* sounds like a blast." She looks over my shoulder, to the house. "Anyway, I think my sweater is here. And some other stuff."

"Oh, um..."

It's not that I want to hide Molly and her family, but I don't have the energy to go through it with Cora. Only a few moments ago it was a peaceful Saturday morning. Now, it's gone.

I get the thorn then wipe my hands on my shorts. "Well, I'll have to look for it, do you need it right now?"

Cora's mouth parts. She glares at me in disbelief before shifting into her world-famous pout. "What, I'm not *allowed* inside now? What's going on, Nat?"

"Nothing is going on; the house is a mess right now. I'll run in, okay?"

She crosses her arms. "It's always a mess."

"Just, stay here. Please."

Cora huffs as I hold my hands up and turn for the door. Inside, Molly and her sisters are at the kitchen table. The girls are coloring pictures, and I catch a whiff of laundry coming from near the garage. The house is not a mess at all, but completely shining from floor to ceiling. I think I even hear the dryer running.

"Hey," I say to the girls.

"Hi Giant."

Molly doesn't look up, and for no reason at all I start explaining myself. "I just need to get her stuff."

"Whose stuff?" Ana asks.

"A friend. I mean, an old friend, or..."

Molly looks up, smirking, taking joy in my struggle with such a simple question.

"Oh," Ana says, getting back to her coloring. While Ashley has drawn daisies and sunflowers, a closer look at Ana's work reveals what looks like Godzilla wielding a sword dripping with what I hope are cherries.

"That's pretty good," I say, because it is. It's also graphic.

Her smile lights up the room. "Thanks. This is a lightsaber."

"Nice."

Ana turns to Molly. "See, *he* likes it."

Molly gives her sister an absent nod. I rush off to find Cora's stuff.

In my room, I sift through the closet and I find the sweater, *a* sweater at least, a pair of flats, tiny shorts, and a Hollins University sweatshirt. It will have to do. I bundle it up, catching a scent of my old life. I realize I still have mulch and dirt all over my hands. Oops.

A quick peek in Mom's door. She's a lump on the bed. A good thing because the last thing I need is Mom in this equation.

I rush down the stairs, round the corner and I'm trying to roll over the sweatshirt I've probably ruined when I find Cora. She roams the kitchen with an air of ownership. Her head is cocked, taking in the scene. Molly sits without expression. Her sisters are smiling.

"You didn't tell me you had houseguests," Cora says, her words oozing with bitchy cheeriness.

"Oh, yeah. Um, this is Molly Martinez."

Cora smiles at me. "We've met."

"And her sisters, Ana and Ashley."

"Hello," Ashley says looking up. "I like your hair."

"Thanks," Cora says, running her hand through it. Then to me, "Can we talk?"

I shrug, still holding the wad of clothes. We head to the living room. Once we're far enough away, Cora takes my arm. "Okay just... what, the absolute—"

"Cora." I drop the clothes on the couch, mulch and all.

"Nat. Do they live here now? Like, *with you?*"

Her voice, the way she says it, it puts heat in my face. I don't care about what she thinks but more what she might say. I shake my head. "I work with Molly. They were evicted, so...keep your voice down, okay?"

"Keep *my voice down?*" She stamps her foot. "Are you kidding me. That's all you have to say? After what we've been through?"

This from the girl who was out of my life the minute I got expelled. When everything collapsed, she pretended like she didn't know. Or she knew but didn't care enough to put her parties on hold and see how I was doing. A few texts and that was it. She didn't even call.

I cut my eyes back to the kitchen. "Cora, come on."

She closes her eyes, crosses her arms and sighs. "Amazing. You're dropping out of school. You're cutting grass. Now what, you're running an immigration center over here?"

"Okay." It's all I can do not to grab her by the arm and escort her out. Instead I march over to the front door. "We're done."

"Excuse me?"

I throw my hands out. "We're done."

"I don't believe this. So you're like, *with* her now?"

In the kitchen, Ana and Ashley break into laughter. Molly shushes them, and it's all I can take, Cora being here. I scoop up the clothes and haul them to the door. Cora follows. "How cute, you two landscaping all day then coming home together."

She follows me down the steps, all the way out to the car, feet stomping and arms swinging. "Seriously, I mean, the future is bright for you, Nat. Really, it is."

I throw the clothes in her car. "Goodbye."

She just stares at me, like she can't believe I'm not begging her to stay like I used to. "You're unbelievable."

"I'll take that as a compliment."

"Don't," she says, getting in her car. She slams the door. Of course Chet and Chase are in their yard, gawking. Cora starts the car, puts it in gear. She sets her sunglasses on her head. "You're a joke."

"Bye Cora."

I get myself together in the backyard. When I get back to the kitchen, Ana stands on the chair and presents her finished drawing. Godzilla and a giant Darth Vader, dueling to the death with lightsabers. Giant Darth Vader looks like he's getting the best of poor Godzilla, who's missing a leg.

My face is hot, my breath still shaky, but I nod and hang the masterpiece on the fridge, right over the school board letter. Molly gets to her feet and starts for the other room.

"Hey." I rub the back of my head where I've broken out in a fresh sweat. It's all too weird, the collision of my old life with my new one. Molly only half turns her face to me. Ashley is asking why her flowers aren't up on the fridge.

Molly snaps at her. "Ash, not now, okay?"

"No, it's fine. Plenty of room." I leap into action, scrambling to find a place near the ice dispenser. The bills fall to the floor and I kick them out of the way. "There."

When I turn around, Molly is gone.

10

Mom wakes up around three that afternoon. Outside her bedroom door sits a neat pile of folded laundry. She picks up a stack of shirts and buries her face in it, looks at me, and smiles.

I have no idea how Mrs. Martinez fixed the dryer, but Mom is thrilled, and inspired too. A rare whirlwind of productiveness gets underway at our house. Mom washes clothes—her real clothes, not nursing scrubs—clothes I haven't seen in months. She cleans her bathroom. A can of Pledge materializes on her dresser. On her bedside table sits a Spanish-to-English book.

I wander around the house, pretending I'm not looking for Molly. I feel this irresistible need to apologize to her, but the door to her room stays shut. I don't want to knock because it would be too awkward. Instead, I shoot some jump shots in the driveway.

A few hours later, Mom's writer nerds start showing up. I help carry in finger foods and drinks and soon, with the house put back together it almost feels like it belongs in the neighborhood. Good old Gary organized this little writer's circle, and he looks proud as he presents Mom with a bottle of wine. She takes off for the kitchen, and I introduce Gary to Ana and Ashley.

Ana leaps onto me and I swing her by the arms. "These two little munchkins are our resident artists."

"Oh, yes. I've heard a lot about you both," he says with a shaky smile. He's obviously still uncomfortable with our situation, but it's sort of hard to look Ana in the eye and not melt. Even when she presents her latest drawing of death and dismemberment.

Soon Mom's party gets popping. Jazz and wine, cheese and crackers, maybe ten writers in the house. There's plenty of drinks to go around, and they all take their time discussing politics and movies with the cocktails before settling in for praise and constructive criticism about their respective works in progress.

I do some blog stalking in my room, but the people-watching downstairs is too tempting. I wander down and hang out in the kitchen, helping where I can. Honestly, I like these little get-togethers. It's nice for Mom to socialize, even if some of these writer types are a bit, um, eccentric. Like Crime-Writer Carol, who does everything besides pinch my cheeks as she marvels over how much I look like my mom. I don't see it, then again, I'm not guzzling sangria.

Gary gets to his feet and clears his throat. He smiles at Mom then clinks his glass to make an announcement. Tonight, he's rocking a yellow button-down shirt and brown corduroys. He takes the floor and, after some throat clearing and hair fixing, says, "I'd like to make a little announcement. My collection of essays, *Impressions of a Dead Capitalist,* has been accepted for publication."

Polite applause. Mom takes his hand and gives him a quick peck on the cheek. Gary's week has been made. They break for drinks and snacks. I find a spot on the couch near Colin, a scruffy poet, and Lydia, a cuteish twenty-something who's been here a couple of times before. Gary dribbles ranch dressing on his shirt. Things get festive.

One of Mom's favorite activities is to have people "bring her writing to life." And it looks as though Gary has been nabbed for the role of Clyde Clisbee, the wacky protagonist from her latest scrawl-in-progress. Gary looks at me and I shrug.

Carol is assigned the role of flirty older woman. Mom directs traffic with the zeal of a dictator. "Okay, now Clyde, you find her at the church, this is just after the raid, and you help her to her feet."

It's hard to watch. I turn for the garage again, still cracking up about Gary in that cowboy hat, when I spot a figure in the doorway. Molly, in a tank top and shorts, looking lost. She motions to the door and whispers, "I was just finishing up the laundry."

The girls must be asleep in their room. I haven't seen Mrs. Martinez, so maybe she's at work. Molly sees me laughing and smiles, her eyes bright and curious as the garage light gleams off her smooth bare shoulders, not that I'm noticing. She leans forward, sensing a conspiracy. "What?"

I take her hand. "Come on, you've got to see this."

She pulls her hand away. "What? No way."

"Trust me."

She looks up suddenly, her face tight. It reminds me of earlier this morning with Cora. But then the living room erupts with laughter, and Molly cranes her neck to look around me, a small smile blooming on her face.

"Okay, what are they doing?"

I lead her to the living room. We peer around the doorway, looking on as Carol sips her sangria from a glass the size of a flower vase, smacks her lips, and holds her hand to her throat in mock terror. "Okay, I'll tell you, just please don't ravage me."

Mom feeds Gary his lines. "You take her hand and say, 'Are you all right, Madam?'"

Gary nods, like a robot. He clears his throat and reads his lines mechanically, "Are. You. All. Right. Madam?"

Molly snorts so loud everyone turns to us. She ducks behind me as Mom spins around. "Nat? Molly?"

Molly digs her fingers into my arm as she peeks out. "Hi Mrs. Reams. I was just..."

"Over here, both of you," Mom snaps then turns to the guests. Gary fixes what hair he has left above his ears. Mom flutters our way, taking Molly by the hand. "This is Molly, isn't she something? She and her family are staying with us!"

The guests all nod and appraise Molly. She stares at the floor as Carol grins at us before she convulses with a hiccup. I roll my eyes, but then Mom yanks me into the room. "Okay, I have just the lines for you two."

I shake my head. "Mom, we're not. No."

Gary laughs, happy to be offstage. Mom looks insulted. "What Nat, you don't want to partake?"

Molly's eyes are moons. She freezes, looking terrified as Mom sweeps us ahead, front and center until I turn and face her. "Mom, no, she doesn't want to..."

To my surprise, Molly recovers with a smile. She stares at me, then turns to Mom. "Sure Mrs. Reams. I'll do a scene."

I shoot her a look. I hadn't pegged Molly for a kiss up. So be it, she has no idea what we're in for. But neither do I, apparently, as Mom, the tyrannical director, suggests one of her little sappy romance scenes.

Colin settles in, getting cozy with Lydia. Molly and I are handed a script, because of course Mom has a script. I take our lines and walk into the ceiling fan chain and everyone laughs. Lydia, having obtained the cowboy hat, is all leg to leg with Colin, whispering in his ear.

I roll my eyes. Colin, amused with my discomfort, tells me to "look alive." Carol knocks back the sangria while Gary sits obediently on the couch with a notebook, like Mom's little puppy dog, dabbing at his shirt and making things worse for himself.

Mom claps and goes on and on about "this next scene," and how she was inspired by whatever the hell she's saying. Molly stands across the room, hair down, hair tie on her wrist, her eyes aimed at me.

At school and at work, Molly is quiet and hardly noticeable. She's been through a ton, obviously, and in my mind she's always the victim, voiceless and vulnerable. But the Molly I'm seeing tonight, right now in the dimly lit room, is fire.

Mom grabs my wrist. "Okay, Nat, you have the role of Bartholomew. You've just returned from Denmark. You've made your millions, but now you yearn for what you sacrificed."

Yearn. I look around the room. "Mom, really?"

Mom shushes me and turns to Molly, clasping her hands and welling up like it's Meryl Streep at the Globes again. "Molly, you, my love, are Victoria. A woman left in the lurch, now engaged to an oil tycoon but still deeply in love with Bartholomew. Your one true love."

"Bartholomew? Come on."

Mom claps. "Now, lines."

The corner lamp struggles against the darkness. Candles, wine, drunk wannabe writers, Colin, reeking of tobacco and cynicism. Molly, across the room, hair spilling to one side, eyes glistening. Fine. I pretend like I'm walking in, see Molly, and jerk back dramatically. "Victoria."

Mom whispers something to Molly, who takes her line with a gasp. "Bartholomew?"

I lumber towards her, reading from my script. "I thought I'd never see you again."

Molly leans forward to read her part. Our forearms touch, which wouldn't be a big deal but for some reason it is. Either way I'm kind of out of breath when she sets her hand on my arm and looks up at me in a way I can't tell if it's real or acting. "Oh Bart, I never, I thought you were gone."

Mom, after a sip of wine, "Pull her close."

Molly scoots up and I pull her in. She's stronger than she looks, more athletic than Cora, and I know it's only some cheesy scene my mom drew up, but my chest tightens. Her hair smells like strawberries. I feel the grooves of muscle in her back and her chest expanding with the giggles she's trying to control. Back to my lines. "No my dear, I was caught up in the war."

Molly goes off script, throwing her head back to Mom. "What war?"

"The Freedom War."

Molly, squinting at Mom, "Huh."

Then, as I'm having all sorts of weird thoughts rush through my mind, two little squeals break us apart. Molly pulls back. She slaps my chest and rolls her eyes. "Bet I know who that is."

We turn to find the two girls, in pajamas, standing in the doorway watching us. Ana looks at her sister. "Molly likes the giant."

Molly and I stand up straight. Molly slides away from me and tugs at her shirt while Mom is up and rushing over to the girls. "Oh, you two little sweethearts."

Molly sets her hair up. "The two of you should be in bed."

There's some color in her cheeks, and I feel it in mine, too. Lydia walks over and everyone fawns over the little girls. Someone whoops in the background, glasses clinking, and the jazz resumes. Molly and I just stand there, staring at the floor, the girls, anything but each other. I can still feel her back in my hand, smell her hair, and I'm wondering what exactly just happened.

11

I t's late, after one in the morning. I'm on the computer stalking my favorite blog. The house is still. Mom is safely tucked away in bed. I'm skimming through *One More Makes Four!*, where Kristen has penned several new posts. Two guest entries I skip through, something about Dannon Yogurt, followed by two soulless pieces about playgrounds with as much personal touch as a Dentist Office Christmas card.

But then, in the weeds, between a Starbucks giveaway and a Charmin challenge, I spot something new. I sit up, spilling milk from the cereal bowl sitting in my crotch. I set it on the coffee table, wiping my face on what I think is a towel but turns out to be Carol-the-Crime-Writer's scarf. Gross, but not gross enough to remove my eyes from the glow of the screen.

Judging by the spew of exclamation points, Kristen is awfully excited about this year's HER TURN conference. At first glance, it looks like just another money-sucking adventure for hopeless bloggers and kid-pimps. Only this one is in Washington D.C., set for July 18th.

I get to my feet and pace, my mind reeling with possibilities. As I already know, Kristen is all about free swag, so nothing new there. But this conference, not too far up the road in only a few days, has my heart pounding. I squeeze my fist, filling it with a faint throb of pain. I sit back down and read it again. All of it, I scroll through the nauseating dribble, Twitter parties and giveaways, branding consultants and wow, they have ambassadors and freaking lifestyle influencers. But none of that matters. What matters is my dad will be only a couple of hours away.

So what does it mean? What do I do? This is the question I'm mulling over when Molly walks in wearing a baggy long sleeve shirt and jogging pants. "Brr, it's freezing in here."

I slap down the laptop. She gives me a look and I realize she probably thinks I was, you know, looking at porn. I hold my hands up. "I wasn't, it was..."

She pretends not to notice and turns for the fridge but stops short. I roll my eyes. "Molly, you live here now, you don't have to ask to open the fridge."

She laughs, points to the crayon drawings. "No, I was looking at the pictures."

"Oh."

I start to turn back around but Molly is still looking at me. "You know, they talk about you nonstop."

I shrug, wiping Fruit Loops from my lap. "Well, I mean, I'm just that cool," I say, gesturing to myself. Molly doesn't laugh. I nod. "It's nice to have a couple of artists in the house, too."

She opens the fridge and grabs a pitcher of water, finds a glass and pours it to the top. She holds it with two hands, leaning on the counter and eyeing me carefully. "So, I was thinking about earlier today."

I shift the laptop. "Oh, that thing with Cora. Wow, what a drama queen, right?"

She closes her eyes and takes a short breath. "No, I mean, yeah. But..."

It takes me a moment to get what she's saying. *Will she report us?*

That's what Molly is talking about. Wow, it's like every time I think I have problems, real problems, double the stakes and it's a typical day in Molly's life. I sit up straight. "Hey, no I don't think she would do anything. It's too much work for Cora, trust me."

She watches me then finally nods. Her shoulders relax some. "So, you can't sleep?"

I shrug and put my arm up when it brushes Carol's scarf again. I jerk away. Molly laughs, then nods towards the computer with a smirk. "Okay, so what *were* you doing?"

I guess I owe her some truths. Besides, after what we've been through, talking about my dad doesn't feel so, confessional. "Okay." I open the laptop and sign back in. "Fine, I'll show you."

She takes a seat in the middle of the couch, beside me, another gust of strawberries. The screen lights up our faces. "My dad's family —his *other* family. Well, his wife has this blog. And, well, I sort of stalk it."

Molly flips her eyes to me but I keep my head down, my face to the screen, glued to the picture of the beaming family staring out at us. It sounds pathetic, because *it is* pathetic. I hate that I can hear my breath quivering.

Molly turns back. "So, this is your sister?" She points to the little blonde chunker.

"Yep, I guess she is."

Molly sips her water. "Wow. She's cute."

I give her a look. "You don't have to lie."

She covers her mouth. A dribble of water spilling through her fingers with her laugh.

I point at her. "Ah, the truth comes out."

She shakes her head. "I choked some," she says, wiping. "I wasn't laughing, I promise."

"I'm on to you, Molly Martinez. You can't fool me."

I scroll down without thinking about what I'm saying. "So, my dad's wife runs all these contests and giveaways. Always out to make a buck on her kid. Their whole life is online, but it's not real, you know. It's…everything is fake. Anyway, when you walked in I was looking it over and, they're coming to DC for this mommy conference thing."

Her smile vanishes. "Wow, really?"

"Yep."

She sits up suddenly, pulls her legs under her. "So, are you going?"

"No, why would I?"

I say it casually, at the same time wondering how she could know that I was really thinking about it, maybe driving up there—the Honda willing—even down to what I'd wear. How it might feel to waltz in there and be like, "Hey Dan, I still exist." Instead, I shake it off. "Wouldn't that be weird?"

Molly's eyes linger on mine for a beat before her gaze returns to the screen. She leans in and looks at my father. "He's tall, too."

"Yeah."

She looks up at me, then to the screen, then me again. "But you look like your mother."

"Funny, I always thought I looked like him," I say, gesturing to the man in the picture. "But that's the second time I've heard I look like my mom in one night."

Molly nods. "You do, your eyes."

I nod, a thousand thoughts in my head but without a word to say. Molly gets to her feet and stretches. "Well, I'm going to bed." She sets the water back in the fridge, turns to me with the dimples, with what I'm quickly discovering is the Molly smirk. "Get some sleep, we've got to finish the yard tomorrow."

"Tomorrow is *Sunday*, as in still the weekend. As in our *other* day off."

"Yep, see you in the morning."

Woodberry College sits in the middle of town, between neighborhoods it's annexed over the years and with a public park on the backside. There's heavy traffic along the dorms, where the parking lots empty out to the main roads. I'm on the push mower, doing the edges while Molly's working the weed whacker, and Virgil mans the Hustler.

Again, my mind roams and draws up fantasies. But where I used to dream about walking on and claiming a spot on the Woodberry basketball team—hitting the game winner at the buzzer then doing the all-conference thing—lately they've been replaced by thoughts on Kristen's blog, or my new roommates, or the way it feels to actually sit and talk to someone about my dad like I did with Molly the other night. It's where my mind is when a car full of kids blows by with a honk of the horn, tossing trash out the passenger window as they fly up the road.

I resist the urge to give them the finger. It's part of the job, people messing with us. Some like to whistle at Molly in passing, probably the reason she wears baggy clothes and tucks her hair in a hat. Others think it's a hoot to toss trash out right in front of where I'm mowing. If

I've learned anything while cutting grass, it's that people in cars are sort of like a comment section online, so long as they don't have to stick around and face the consequences of their actions, they're left free to be complete jackasses.

But it's clear the next car isn't just messing with us. It's slowing, circling around, pulling in, stopping. And it's not your typical Scion full of college kids, either. It's an older style Cutlass, low, shiny, with huge rims and tinted windows. It's a car I recognize from Lafayette Estates.

Molly stops cold and stares at them. I release the lever and the Toro falls silent. A short but solid guy emerges from the car. Two, then three, now four Latino guys.

The driver is all smiles as he approaches Molly. It's easy to see they know each other, but the guy looks like a real jerk, especially with the cocky grin on his face.

They kind of surround Molly, who's not enjoying it and looks ready to put the weed-whacker to good use. Without thinking, I hustle over and one of them turns my way as I approach.

"What's up guys?" I sound dumb. Molly whips her face to me, a slight shake of the head, before she's back to taking them straight on, unflinching and emotionless. It's not the Molly from school or even the one from my house, not the one from Mom's writing party the other night. This girl is hardened, ready for war.

The guy with the cocky grin looks me up and down. He's got three lines parting his eyebrows. He nods at Molly. "Just checking up on our girl."

Our girl. I turn to Molly who only glares at the guy. I shrug, trying to keep things casual even though I feel my pulse in my temples. "Yeah, well, we're kind of busy right now."

I tower over these guys with their baggy clothes and sneakers, but the dude hanging back has a neck like a log and looks like he'd love a chance to cut me down to size. The other three look content to grin and sneer, like villains in a bad movie. The guy with the eyebrows speaks again. "This your new man, Molly?" He says her name like *Malee*. He turns to me. "Hey, you the guy with the car, right?"

"The car?" I manage.

He scratches the scraggily hair on his chin. "Yeah," he says with a laugh. "Had some trouble with the window, no?" He smiles at Molly, who drops her head, eyes focused on the end of the trimmer. He clicks his teeth, ignoring me now, shaking his head. "The landlord, he tossed all your things on the curb. You should have listened to me."

He seems to take pleasure in delivering the news. And Molly, who didn't seem to care about her possessions when we were moving, flinches with each word. The guy turns to me, then back to Molly. "Just thought you'd want to know."

The Hustler goes silent. Virgil comes plodding up to the party, and for once I'm glad to see the guy on a job. "What's going on, guys? We got grass to cut."

Traffic starts and stops, people watching from the windows. But even with big Virgil panting down our necks, these guys never look away from Molly, who hasn't moved or spoken. She hasn't breathed from what I've seen. The guy with the grin backs away, staring. "Okay, Molly. *Ten cuidado amigo.*"

They do some more sneering and Virgil and I sit there burning in the sun without a clue what is going on or what any of them are saying. Molly only glares at them.

They pile back in the car, revving the engine and being obnoxious. I'm flustered, but it's nothing too serious until Log-neck points at me and winks. I wink back, although my knees are rubber. My mouth has gone dry.

Virgil, the loon, steps forward. "Go on, get out of here."

My chest heaves, lungs sucking for air that's not making the trip. My vision blurs, and I'm about to puke when the guy points his finger like a gun directly at me and pretends to pull the trigger. I flinch as the car grumbles and they pull out and onto the road. When they're gone, I collapse against a tree.

"Molly, what the...?"

She stares at the curb as they drive off. Her face is like a stone, and only when the car is out of sight does she chance a look up to Virgil, who's huffing around and shaking his head. "Going to lose this account with this crap."

Account? I'm ready to call it a day. But Molly, the girl I've seen playing princess with her little sisters, stands defiantly, watching the street as Virgil stalks off towards his mower.

When Virgil is gone, Molly wipes her forehead and starts for the weed whacker. I'm sitting under the tree, knees pulled to my chest. Whatever my stomach is sending up burns the back of my throat.

Molly halfway turns to me. "Are you okay, Nat?"

She's asking *me.* I attempt to get to my feet, but it's like my leg muscles have been replaced with chewed gum. The gun gesture, it leaves me unnerved, like jelly.

She gives me a small smile. I get myself up and follow her over to a tree near a brick wall of the entrance way, hidden from traffic and somewhat shaded. I open my mouth a few times but no words make the trip. I need some water.

Molly's smile evaporates. She waves her hand in the direction the Cutlass went screaming up the road. "They're mostly talk."

Mostly. I wipe my face. It's in the high eighties, but my sweat-soaked shirt is cool on my back. I look at Molly. "What do they want?"

Virgil makes a pass our way, looking ticked because we're not back on the job. Molly picks up the weed whacker. "Do you think Virgil's going to fire me for this?"

I stretch, getting some feeling back in my legs. "*That's* what you're worried about?"

Molly stops mid-pull on the weed whacker, raises her head and nods. She yanks the cord again and it fires up. She looks back at me one last time, then she's off.

At lunch, I ask questions. Molly reluctantly fills me in. "Last year we were about to be evicted, and so I borrowed some money."

"Okay." I wonder if she's telling me everything. "So, what did they want in return?"

Molly hits me with a razor-sharp glare. "What is that supposed to mean?"

I shrug. I'm not sure what I mean, so I shut up.

She pulls her hair back. She hasn't touched the sandwich her mother made this morning. I've already destroyed mine. She takes a breath. "I was going to pay them when I could, but then the power got cut off so... I guess I still owe them."

"You think, I mean, if you pay them will they leave you alone?"

She shrugs. She has no idea and she doesn't seem too worried about it. She's more worried about Virgil, between the time off and now this, she's sure he's going to fire her.

I don't know why she cares about this job so much, I mean, Mom doesn't want money. Maybe she wants to save. Maybe it's pride. Maybe it's the same reason I don't quit and give up.

With my brain working again, I tell Molly I'll handle Virgil. She looks skeptical, but I assure her, as the person who got her this job, I should be the one to save it, too.

For the rest of the day I'm checking over my shoulder, looking for bad guys in loud cars. Guys with guns, maybe, or knives, or who knows? I'm trying to come up with something to say to Virgil. Something to keep him from firing Molly.

As soon as we're back at the garage, I ask him if we can talk in the shop. He gives me a dead stare, like he knows everything I'm going to say. Still, he motions for the shop and I follow him back and shut the door.

"Don't fire her, it's not her fault."

Virgil turns around and gets right in my face. "No? It's not? Nat, some gang bangers coming around, harassing us." He points at the door. "Because of her."

"She needs this job, Virgil."

He stares at me for ten seconds, breathing loud through his nose. The odor floating off him is ripe and overwhelming. Virgil's collar has its five o'clock sag to it, rung out with sweat and grass. He turns for the sink. "I could've told you this would happen."

"Told me *what* would happen?"

He turns to me, hands smeared, dripping, levels me with a stare. "I'm not stupid, Nat. She's nice to look at, but she's trouble."

Seriously? Not this again. "Virgil."

"And now you've gone and moved her in with you. Could have told you that was a dumb thing to do, too. You need to think with your brain instead of your—"

"Virgil. Listen to me."

He puffs out his cheeks, lifts his Cargill hat, soggy from sweat, sweeps his hand through his hair. If Virgil's going to fire Molly, he should at least have all the facts. I press on. "Look, she owes them some money. For rent."

He tears into the old fridge, bottles clanging around when he shuts the door. The old fridge may have been white a lifetime ago, but it's tanned to a brown and smeared from all the dirt and grass and grease. He hands me a water, keeps a Diet Coke for himself. The guy probably drinks ten Diet Cokes a day.

He snaps the top and takes down half in two pulls, then leans back at the sink, calmer than I would have guessed. "Nat."

"That's it," I say, like I really know the whole story. But I believe Molly. I really do. It's clear Virgil does not.

"It's a sad story. Really it is. But I'm a business owner. Not a charity. This ain't some sanctuary city."

I try not to roll my eyes. Last fall, Virgil got big into talk radio so now everything is political with him. It's laughable, because he's the one who hired her, pays her under the table, and I'm guessing he short-changes her wages. I keep my voice low. "I'm asking for me, Virg. As a favor."

It's my way of saying, "If you fire her you fire me."

"Nat. Let it go." He pounds his soda and gives me a grin. "I know you mean well. I know you want to help this *Chica*, be her savior and all, but—"

"I'm going to help a friend, if that's what you mean. Yeah."

"What are you going to do, Nat? Pay off some thugs?"

I shrug. Virgil steps back, all smug. "Let me guess, you're going to quit if I fire her, right?"

I stare at the floor. Virgil sighs, has a talk with the ceiling. I pounce. "She's got two little sisters. You should see her with those girls. She's smart too, honors student, Virgil, even with all that kind of stuff going on in her life."

Right then, as we stand in the dank garage, I almost tell him about Mr. Meyers. But I can't. Just thinking about it makes me cringe. I hear Molly pleading with him to stop, her voice cracking because she might have to let him...how she's always had to let people have their way because she can't stand up or speak up or even go on a field trip.

Virgil watches it on my face. I shake it off and try again. "I want to help her mother. Help her family. Is that so bad?"

He points at me. "Don't start that, Nat. *We are the World* and all that. It's only going to get us shot cutting grass."

I shrug. Virgil does more huffing and puffing. Then he says, "If it happens again. I'm sending both of you packing and I'm calling the cops. I'm too old for this. I cut grass, Nat. I don't run a support group for illegals."

"She's not *illegal*," I blurt out, because she's not. She hasn't broken any laws. She's only trying to live.

Virgil turns and stares at me. I stand firm and let it sink in. I know Virg likes Molly. And we both know he'll never find someone who works the way she does. We also both know he'll never call the cops because if he does, he'll have a lot of explaining to do. Otherwise he would have fired her on the spot today.

More huffing. "I can't believe your mother let them live with you."

His voice goes soft when he talks about her. I throw Virgil a bone, using my mom as bait. It's gross, but I'm desperate. "I think it will be good for her."

He stops just as he cracks into his second Diet Coke, like he can't believe my nerve. I watch the foam erupt from the tiny crack in the lid and drip on the concrete. "Oh, so you're not only helping some illegals out, but your dear mother, too?"

I roll my eyes. "Come on, Virg. Why do you say that stuff?"

"What? The truth? I call it like I see it."

"Illegals? Molly hasn't done anything wrong."

He wipes the back of his neck, then crushes the soda and burps. "You got it bad for this girl, huh?"

I start to protest but he's not finished. And since I'm in no position to walk away I lean back on the oil-stained plywood table where a chainsaw is splayed out.

Virgil keeps up with the head shaking. "When I was seventeen, I spent my summer drinking beer and chasing girls. I thought I knew it all back then, you know? Had all the answers. Then I turned to the hard stuff. Cocaine and all that. But it was the liquor I couldn't stay away from. It was the booze that stole my family."

I've heard Virgil's story of drugs and addiction and AA meetings so many times I can taste the stale coffee in the church basement. Instead, I focus on his various calendars, all smudged and curling at the corners. He has a golf one, a Husqvarna one. A Viagra one that's from 2008 he finds hilarious. He must know I'm getting bored because he expedites the lesson.

"What I'm saying is it took me until I was thirty, when I flat-lined at a stop light, before I realized I didn't know a thing about this life. I was a flea on the world's balls. Nobody cared whether I drank myself to death or if I climbed out of my hole. It was up to me."

For another twenty minutes, I listen to Virgil's greatest hits. He calls me snowflake. Bed-wetter. Bleeding Heart. He keeps saying things about me keeping it in my pants. But in the end, after enduring Virgil's recovery saga, he cuts me a check for a thousand bucks, and I make him promise Molly's job is safe.

For now.

13

———————

I n the car, on the way home, I'm talking fast, in fragments, trying to explain to Molly how I talked Virgil into a check for a grand. I skim over the part about how he's going to dock us twenty-five bucks a week for the rest of our lives.

Molly does Molly. She stares ahead without a word, without a smile, without a blink as the bag in the window flaps along in the back. I ask if she wants to go by the trailer, see what's left of her belongings, but she only shakes her head, chews on her nails. She offers nothing.

It's been a rough day for both of us, but more for her than me. I clench my fist, tighter and tighter, willing the soreness into my knuckles. "You think the girls caused any trouble?"

Molly nods. I look at her and smile. "Maybe they helped Mom with her makeup. It could only help, right?"

"Nat."

"Yeah?"

I glance over to her. To her eyes like mirrors, no longer absorbing but reflecting. She shakes her head, takes a deep breath. "The money. After we pay them back, then I owe you even more than I do now."

"Huh? No." My shoulders slump, because I see what she means —even if it's not like that. Damn. I'm just trying to solve problems here, because apparently, I can't solve my own. "No, you don't. You don't owe me. We pay these guys and that's it."

She closes her eyes, rubs her forehead. "It's never over. Now I owe you for...for being in the chem lab that day, for giving me a place to live." Her hands fall in her lap. Trembling. She's about to lose it. "And now, for this."

Her face flushes. She turns to the window, then back to me. "If it weren't for me, you'd be in school this year, playing basketball. Not paying five hundred dollars back to your boss." Her voice cracks. "You'd have your scholarship."

I stop at a red light, start fooling with the radio, the lump in my chest climbing to my throat, my nose, between my eyes. I take a breath. "Maybe. But that sounds boring, right? This, though. *This* is a learning experience."

She shakes her head, her eyes glossy. "You drive me crazy sometimes."

"Yeah?" I give her my best smile. "I get that a lot."

She rolls her wet eyes, purses her lips to squash the budding dimples of her smile, and suddenly, thankfully, the mood is lighter.

"What?" I ask.

"Nothing, just...your smile. It's the jerk one you always had on your face after you'd score."

I shift in my seat. My smile? "Wait, what? You went to the games?"

She shrugs. Blinks a few times to clear the mist. "Mmm, hmm."

I look at the road, then back to her. "I can't tell if you're being serious right now."

She chews on her lip, maybe to stop the breakaway smile from completely evolving. Then she's over it, smiling fully, a quick wipe of the eyes as she sits straighter, her voice lighter. "Well, I know you don't utilize your high-low game enough."

I shift my body to get a better view of her. "Um, *what?*"

Behind us, someone honks and I get moving, happy to be talking about something, anything other than favors or owing people. Anything but that day in chem lab.

Molly looks ahead and nods, turns to me, her hair loose and falling over her face. She fiddles with the hair tie in her hands. "Like in state playoffs last year, against Paulson. They played zone, right? The free throw line extended was there the whole game."

My mouth is open. Hanging open. I grip the steering wheel. The worn rubber is beginning to peel and sticks to my palms. I wipe it off on my pants. "We lost because DeShaun went cold. They trapped us and we turned the ball over fifteen times. How do you—"

She throws her hair back and wraps the tie around her ponytail with practiced ease. "Well, I guess. But they only trapped after they scored. And at the other end, you were buried down at the baseline nearly the whole game. If your coach had told you to flash up top, it would have drawn them out—you would have had that shot all game. And you like that shot, right?"

I shake my head, thinking back to the game. Paulson did run a zone. It took some adjusting because nobody had run zone on us all year. "How in the world do you know this?"

She pulls her knees up, sets her chin down. "My dad liked basketball. Okay, *loved* basketball. He was always talking about the Bulls, Michael Jordan and all that. I just kind of absorbed it."

"I had no idea you went to our games."

"Most. I even brought Ashley to a couple of them. She whined about popcorn the whole time. But I saw enough to know you can hit that shot. And if they'd come up, it would have opened things up underneath."

I look at the house in a daze, because we're home even though the whole ride was a blur. The lawn looks good but the screen over the garage is busted. The siding needs to be cleaned. All I'm thinking about is Molly the basketball fan. Amazing. Seriously, this girl is one big surprise. "Do you play ball or just coach?"

She shrugs. "I'm okay."

Enough. I need some answers. Shaking my head, I start the car. Molly turns to me as I shift into reverse. "What are you doing?"

"What do you mean?" I motion to the goal above the car in the driveway. I'm backing out to give us some room. "I need to see what you got."

Her eyes go wide. "I have to take care of the girls. Mom works tonight."

"Great excuse, really. But I need to see your game."

I hop out and scoot around the car, open her door. She looks back to the house. "I can't right now. I have to do dinner and tuck-ins."

It melts me a little to hear it. I nod, wanting to hug her more than ever, instead I take a step back. "Ah, saved by the tuck-ins."

"Yep," she says, getting her things and smirking again. "Maybe another day I can help you with your game."

"Maybe."

We start for the porch when Chet and Chase bust out of their house, football in hand. They're arguing about a catch when they see us and stop talking.

Molly looks at me. "At least we're inconspicuous."

Chase and Chet scatter out to the street and start tossing the ball around.

I flap the check in my hand. "So, tomorrow we'll cash this, okay?"

She nods. "Look, Fabio, he doesn't—"

"Wait. Whoa, hold on. His name is Fabio?"

"Yeah, why?"

"Nothing." I look down, kick a pebble off the walkway. "Just, wow."

Inside, we're greeted by the thumps of tiny feet. The girls brush past Molly and Ana presents a picture. Godzilla has split the Death Star in two.

"Oh, this is gorgeous. I love the details."

Molly stares at me. Our moms come in from the kitchen. It's weird, because the house holds the thick aroma of dinner, and the girls are giggling. Because my mom's not up in her room asleep. It's weird and different and kind of nice too.

"Hey guys, we're doing grilled cheese and soup tonight." Mom gestures to Molly's mom. "Maria cooked so we're safe."

I look at Molly, who drops her things and scoops up Ana. She kisses her on the cheek. "Were you a good girl today?"

Ana beams. She sees me smiling at her and buries her head in Molly's neck. Whatever Virgil thinks about Molly or what's going on, he's wrong. I'm right.

And I'm glad I did what I did today.

14

After a shower I find the laptop and hop online, leeching off the Andrews' WIFI to scan through my favorite blog. Nothing new but a diaper giveaway. Mom calls me down for dinner and I shut the laptop and close my eyes for a second, thinking how weirdly wonderful it is to hear her do that.

It's nuts with six people at the dinner table. The girls talk over each other, bicker over ketchup, soup, milk. Mrs. Martinez leaps to her feet any time Mom gets up from the table. Molly and I exchange embarrassed looks. In short, it is so much better than my nightly showdowns with Mom.

There's a constant noise in the house now. Laughter, television, music, even the occasional crying. It covers the loneliness. Even with all the uncertainty—the house, the bills, and the school thing—it isn't until now that I realize how much the silence was killing me.

I mean, I'm not fooled. Mom isn't suddenly fixed. There's a hint of booze on her breath and she's still talking about her terrible *One Moon* story, but it's different somehow. She's upbeat but not in the clouds, dreaming but not delusional. Maybe these two little girls are fairies after all, because they've cast some sort of spell on my mom.

She's attuned to them. She's lesson planning, workshopping, scheduling these little activities. Yesterday they were in the backyard searching for four leaf clovers. I watched from the window for twenty minutes. It was great.

After dinner, I insist on giving Mrs. Martinez a ride to work. On the way out to the Stay 'N Go, a low-slung, two-story hotel off the expressway, she spends most of the ride thanking me. I'm tempted to ask her about Fabio and those guys, but it seems like Mrs. Martinez already has plenty enough to worry about.

"I get paid on Friday," she says in a heavy accent.

I wave her off. "No, it's fine, really." Then I feel bad for disregarding her offer so quickly.

Where Molly is bilingual—she can turn it on and off like a switch —and her sisters are mostly English speaking, Mrs. Martinez struggles with the most basic English and the daily customs I take for granted.

She shakes her head, as though charity is unacceptable, and I decide not to argue with her. The sky burns orange and crimson behind the trees. After a mile or so of silence, I attempt to make small talk with Maria, but it's hard to find common ground. "So, Ana is some artist, huh?"

She nods, gives me a big proud smile. "Oh yes, she is something, that one." Then her eyes come alive, like she's divulging a big secret. "But Molly is the artist. I hope she will keep," she makes brush strokes in the air with her hands, "helping with her."

I turn to her, taking in this new information. "Molly is the artist?"

"Oh, yes. You see her paintings?"

Molly the basketball fan. Molly the honor roll student. Molly the artist? I nearly miss the exit, braking hard, metal grinding as the car behind us honks and jumps over to the next lane. I smile at Mrs. Martinez to put her at ease. "The ones we moved, those were Molly's paintings? Like, she painted them?"

Mrs. Martinez nods proudly, a small dimply, creased smile. It reminds me of her daughter. I'm shaking my head as we pull to the curb, thinking, what does this girl not do well?

Mrs. Martinez unbuckles her seatbelt. "Thank you for the ride," she says, then turns back, almost shyly. "Give her time. Since her father, Molly has a hard time trusting people."

"Yeah," I say, flustered, still thinking about those paintings. Whatever happened to her father? "So um, what time should I pick you up?"

She bundles her things together in a cloth grocery bag. She looks up at me, kind of like Molly does, eyes taking in my face and thoughts. "It will be late," she says. "Don't you worry, okay?"

Before I can answer, she closes the door and hustles off for the Stay 'N Go. I wait for her to get inside the drably brick building, wondering how in the world she does this all night. How many times have I passed housekeepers, hotel staff, landscapers, and never once thought about how they were human beings with hopes and dreams or remarkable kids who paint and laugh on occasion and dare me to earn their smiles? Then I drive away.

The sun has sunken to a glow and the heat isn't so miserable. The car jounces and squeaks, and once again I drive past the mattresses and litter boxes, the flattened plastic bottles and grocery bags and scattered cigarette butts.

Welcome to Lafayette Estates. Again.

I flip my eyes left and right, looking for trouble on either side. A mound of belongings are piled at the edge of Molly's yard. A ratty couch, some rolled up rugs, folded over boxes and clothes. On the other side, laying on its side, is Molly's easel. I pop the trunk and hop out.

Next door the music thumps. Across the drive, a lamp illuminates the rebel curtain. My breath is cut short. The last thing I need is for Molly's "friends" to show up or some loon to bust out and start with the rock throwing again.

I'm at the easel in three steps. The legs are loose at the joints, but I get it folded up and wedged into the trunk. I find a few supplies.

Brushes, chalk, some pencils and charcoal that's spilled over into the gravel.

Then I'm just scooping crap out of the pile. An old stroller. A board game with a flimsy top, pieces spilling everywhere. Little girl shirts, toys, towels, dolls, whatever I can grab. I'm moving like a madman as I shove it in the trunk, slam it shut, then leap back into the car and tear off.

Back at the house I back into the driveway and unload it all into the garage. I hear the girls giggling in the bathroom, the sound of splashing. Molly directing things. It makes me smile.

Another trip out and I run into my favorite twin. "Hey, Nat."

"What's up, Chase."

He eyes the stroller dangling from my hand. "Nothing much. Did you guys, like, get a maid?"

I stop and laugh. "Uh, no."

"So then who are those people? I mean, that woman? Those girls?"

I look past him, to see if maybe Mr. Andrews set him up for this, but Chase shrugs. "My dad's out of town. Again."

"Oh, well, we're just having some friends stay with us."

"Oh."

I start for the garage and Chase follows me in, where he picks up one of the four basketballs in the corner. "Dad says you're not playing ball this year."

A flash of anger hits. "Yeah? Your dad sure seems to know a lot about me."

His eyes fall to the ground and I let out a sigh. I didn't mean to snap at him, as far as twins go, they're not exact copies of one another. Chet is a jerk, but Chase takes things to heart. Now he's staring at his feet, holding the ball. I nod my head at him. "Hey, look. I'm sorry, it's just, it's complicated."

He nods, then his face lights up. "Hey, you got time for a game?"

The hope in his eyes, the feel of a basketball. I flip the light switch on, illuminating the driveway. "Yeah sure, let's go."

15

I give Chase some open jumpers. He misses the first few before he finds his rhythm, hitting the next two before missing. I snatch the rebound and shoot him a smile. The rule is I play left-handed, since I'm right-handed. I clear it out and he rushes over to play me tight on defense. The other rule, apparently, is that Chase is allowed to smack and claw and otherwise beat the crap out of me. We used to play me against Chet and Chase, but since Chet is a moody little jerk it's just Chase and me.

Chase lunges for the ball, and I take it in for an easy score when a car pulls up. Cora's car. I miss my next shot because I'm not looking.

She parks on the curb and makes her way up the driveway with a nice little bounce she's perfected. She tosses back her sandy blonde hair, throwing her chest out. Even in the dark, she's got it working now, as she shows up unannounced, just after Chase celebrates his bank-shot from the sidewalk.

The phone is pressed to her cheek as she scrunches up her nose and waves, like the other day never happened. Chase watches closely as she approaches, swishing her hips and talking, rocking those mom-jean shorts girls love and guys hate.

But she's pulling it off. She takes me in for a hug, hanging on to my arm as I'm wondering if she remembers calling me a joke the other day. She mouths "sorry" and gets back to her crisis. "Really? He *said* that?"

With Cora, it's a game of compromises, suffering through all the manufactured drama for those rare glimpses of reality. There were a few times, when we were alone, where we had real conversations. Few people know this because Cora works hard to hide it, but she's smart. She wants to study to be a marine biologist. That's why she's going to ODU in the fall. At least that used to be the plan. It's hard to keep up.

"Okay, call me later, let me know...okay...bye."

Her sky-blue eyes scan me. I've taken my shirt off because it's muggy and I'm sweating. She gives me an approving smile but then she holds up the phone. "Maureen is freaking out."

I motion with my head how there's a kid around before she launches into some tirade, but Chase only snorts.

"Oh, I'm sorry," she says, head cocked and smiling. Chase stares, a goofy smile on his face.

"So uh, what's going on?" I say, meaning, *what are you doing here?*

Cora reaches out and runs a finger down my arm. "Wow, look at you. All tan, and your hair, it's starting to curl." She still has my arm as she leans in, craning her neck. I pull away.

"Hold on, wait. I thought I was a joke."

She smiles, waving it off. "Maybe I missed you." She holds onto my arm, smiling wider and scooting up next to me.

Chase, who's twelve, cannot adequately take a hint. He stands and goggles. Cora looks over the car, trunk popped, little girl clothes spilling out of a trash bag. The window. She gives me a look. "So uh, what's up with the car?"

"That's um, well, it's..."

Inside the house, a Pterodactyl shrieks. We turn just as the front door swings open, and there's my mother tearing out of the house, a blur of neon yellow nursing scrubs. Behind her are the two pajama clad little girls, the source of the screaming.

I can't help laughing as Mom does a lap around the dogwood tree and Ana and Ashley, arms up, give chase. Cora is not so amused. "What the hell?"

Her face goes tight as Molly appears at the door, laughing and completely into whatever game they're playing, until she sees us. Her face drops and she calls after the girls.

Ana sees me and starts in on her favorite game. "The giant! The giant. Must eat the giant."

They change course and start for me, Molly calling after them. "Ana, no. It's time for bed."

Ana and Ashley bolt over to us and stop. "Hello," Ana says to Cora. Then to me. "Is this your girrrlfriend?"

"Ana!" Molly rushes over. She's talking bedtimes, wearing a tank and jogging pants. It's sort of obvious to anyone they live here.

Molly doesn't look at me or even acknowledge Cora. Ashley joins in with the teasing. *The giant has a girlfriend. The giant has a girlfriend.*

Suddenly I'm acutely aware of how I'm not wearing a shirt. Again, Cora slides closer to me, and, always inappropriate, she sets her hand on my bare stomach. "We're just good friends, now."

I slide away. Molly finally looks at me, and her eyes linger for a moment and I want to tell her about the easel. How she can use the garage to paint. But it seems dumb now, with Cora standing next to me. Molly takes her sisters and drags them inside just as Mom makes her enters-stage-left and we plunge into Act III of the Make-Nat-Uncomfortable dinner theater production.

"Hi Cora, how are you, sweetie?"

Mom and Cora hug. Cora plays up the sweet girl role. "Hi Mrs. Reams, it's so good to see you."

"And you, dear," she says, stepping back to take Cora in. "You are just adorable." She turns to me for confirmation. "Isn't she, Nat."

I slide into my t-shirt. "Yep."

Mom waves me off just as Mrs. Andrews steps out to call Chase, whose eyes are glued to Cora, more specifically her chest. Mrs. Andrews calls him again, but he makes no visible means to hide his staring. Cora brushes her hair back and reaches out to him. "I think you're being called home, cutie."

Chase's eyes bulge. It's clear the kid's night is made. He nods several times and backs away. "Chase, the ball." I clap my hands but he merely drops it and hustles off, no doubt going to brag to his brother about what has just happened to him.

Mom begs off, heading inside to check on things. Cora sighs and pouts and I'm about to come up with an excuse to leave when she takes my hand, gives me a little smile, and leads me into the garage.

"You could have left your shirt off."

"Cora." I look at the easel, my two worlds colliding, her breath on my neck.

"Hey, you."

"Cora."

"Shh," she says, and I give up. I can't help it. It's been a while since I've had much, uh, interaction with anyone. Ever since I was expelled, it's like I've been living on Mars. And most of the time I'm okay with it, but now, her warm breath, her lips on my ear, well...

She backs me onto my dad's old reading chair that's been stored away because I guess my mom thinks it's haunted. I want Cora to leave, I really do. But I haven't exactly had company in a while and so, with her on my neck, my hands start to do things they used to do with Cora. They reach for her hips, instinctively. Her breath catches in my ear. It's familiar, all of it, her mixture of smells. The fresh jasmine mixed with the faint scent of tobacco and cinnamon. How her mouth finds mine.

I give in. I kiss her back. Because I miss doing anything I used to do before my life became a dead zone.

Yelps inside. I tense, and Cora backs off, smiling, her hair falling over her blue eyes. She's teasing me. Although maybe Cora's not the only drama queen in our relationship. Maybe it's the reason we've lasted so long, on and off, because we thrive on the drama.

She slides her hands up my arms, throws a leg over me and I take her hips again. She's a lion tamer, toying with her captive. She leans in, as I'm stretched out on the chair with her straddling me, kissing me.

She slides up my chest and whispers in my ear. "I've missed this."

I nod. It's what we used to do when we were alone. She leans into me again, kissing my neck, her hand sliding up my shirt. I grip the rail, and for a second, it's like old times again. Then things get weird.

It's not weird because I'm kissing Cora like I have hundreds of times before, but, it's that...I'm kissing Molly. It's Molly's hands on my face. Her sharp brown eyes burning into mine. Her rare smile in the car. I see her arms through the grass trimmings and haze. The way her face lit up when we were talking about basketball. I'm still with Molly when Cora pulls away from me.

"Nat." She looks confused, wounded, her eyes still wide but her tone getting sharp. "Nat, what is it?"

I shake my head. "Cora, I can't. I can't do this."

Two seconds for her to switch gears, to roll her eyes and shove off me. She fixes her shirt then drops her head to pout. I reach for her, but my hand doesn't make the trip. I'm still shaken up by what happened. I let out a deep sigh. "Cora, look."

She throws her hands in her lap and hangs her head. Sometimes I get the feeling Cora is acting for a studio audience only she can see. In her best soap opera whisper, she says, "Do you know how many people ask me about you? About..." She shoots me a wet glare and drops it.

"What?"

"Like, if you're crazy..." She shakes her head, as though my sanity is too painful to think about.

I can't help laughing. "Crazy? Like what, I'm some raging mental case?"

She breaks out of her little act, straightening, nodding at the door to the house. "You did attack a teacher."

"Look, I didn't..."

"And what exactly *is* going on?" She looks around the garage. "What is all this? Are you like, hooking up with that girl now?"

It's like she's ripped into my head. I run my hand through my hair. "Cora, what are you talking about? Molly? Seriously?"

My voice isn't into it. It's weak, flimsy. Because yes, Molly. Seriously. Talking about her after whatever just happened feels like a confession.

She stands up, adjusts her bra straps, her shirt and shorts. She throws her hair back and goes for her phone. "Okay, I'm leaving."

And she leaves.

I sit in my father's chair, in our dark garage, thinking about crazy. How my new life and old life don't mix. How people find it so strange that Molly, her mother, her sisters, live with us. Like there's a set of rules Mom and I never received. Rules we're not supposed to break. All of this is flooding my mind when I call out to Cora. Not *for* her, but *to* her, to make sure she won't say anything. But Cora simply tosses up her hand and gets into her car and backs out. Then she's gone.

And I stay. In my father's chair, in the dark garage with the boxes and broken easel and the baby carriage. Alone with everyone's throwaways.

16

Virgil eyes his watch as Molly and I pull into the lot the next morning. Things are quiet in the car. Molly hasn't said two words, besides, "mm hmm," since breakfast. She's out the door almost before I can park, hustling to the trailer to fill gas cans.

It's been like this since last night. After Cora left, I told her about the easel in the garage and she rolled her eyes. "You went back? Are you trying to lose all of your windows?"

Some thanks I get.

Virgil maps out the day. I'm happy to hear I'll be working alone, to give Molly some time to get over whatever is bothering her. To stay away from Virgil, who keeps giving me this *told you so* smirk. It's all starting to piss me off.

I hit the Hills with the sun on my back, throwing myself into the work. I clear my thoughts and simply push and pull and absorb the instant gratification of cutting down the high stalks. I've managed to put the Cora thing away, convinced myself she'd probably already forgotten as soon as she drove away. But the school board bears down on me. Because what happens then, after they go through with the expulsion? Night school? GED? Virgil said there's not enough work during the winter months. I guess I'll be job hunting.

Somehow there's still room for the pipe dream of driving to D.C. and...what? Confronting? Surprising? Spying on my dad at the convention? From what I've read, the whole fam is tagging along. One more makes four. It makes me want to punch something. Then again, look where *that* got me.

Within it all lies Molly. The more I try to help her the more she blames me for everything. Or doesn't blame me but resents my help. What is she mad about, anyway? Cora? Maybe she just doesn't want Cora around her sisters. She's so damn protective of them. Of everything.

Tired of guessing, I grab a burger and fries for lunch, alone, checking my phone for updates, soaking up info about the Her Turn website.

The event is booked to the gills. Speakers from all over the country. Raffles. Major sponsors. Martha, The View, Amazon, Cook at Home. Disclaimers for days. Kristin is all over it.

Like us here, or here, or here.

If nothing else, she's determined to make this being-a-mom thing really pay off. And the more I read her sappy posts about the new baby—technically my new half-sister—the more I want to drive up there and shatter this perfect-family-online-image she's created.

All of this would be easier if I was still the all-area basketball player instead of troubled loser. I could show up, flash a smile, and I bet Dad would take me in, introduce me to people, brag about my stats and where I'm planning to go to school.

Have you signed up for the newsletter?

When I get back to the shop, after a half an hour of wallowing in fantasyland, Molly is struggling to unload the Toro. I run over to help her out and I'm surprised when she lets me. I yank it down and lug it to the shop and come back for the push mower, where she offers a quick thanks, wiping her brow.

I start to say something like, "Oh you're talking to me now," but before I can she takes a breath and says, "Look, I'm sorry I was short this morning. I just, I'm really protective of my sisters, okay?"

"I figured," I say, shrugging like I hadn't thought about it. I go to grab the mower, but Molly isn't finished. Her eyes go left, right, everywhere but up to me. "Look, it was sweet of you to go back for my things. Kind of stupid, but sweet, too."

"You're um, welcome?"

She stares at her old running shoes, the soles and sides slick with grass stains. "I just, I don't know how to handle this." She tosses her hands up, finally looking into my eyes. "You know, moving in, your house. It's going to take some getting used to, living with you and your mom, you know?"

I shrug. "Well, *I'm* still trying to get used to living with my mom. But I don't know. She seems to be doing better recently."

She crosses her arms. A clump of hair falls in her face and she blows it away. "And you?"

"And me what?"

"How are you doing, Nat?"

I throw my hands out, put on a big smile. "I'm great. Just wonderful."

I laugh it off, but her face doesn't crack. She holds me with her gaze, like she knows she's the only person who has asked me that question since everything happened. Like she knows I'm a fraud, running around shrugging and being a smartass when really I'm terrified because I'm about to lose the last thing I had left. And so I turn and shrug and shake and try to get away from her eyes because her eyes make me want to confess things, like how I was thinking about her when I was kissing Cora.

We're still standing there, facing off, when good old Virg comes shuffling out of the garage with a burp. "Hey," burp, hiccup, belch. "'Scuse me. You know where the two-cycle is?"

Molly runs up on the trailer, grabs it and hands it to him. It gives me a minute to get myself together. He burps again, like he's been hit with a stun gun. "Damn, 'scuse me, thanks."

He plods back to the shed. I raise a brow and hook my thumb. "And that guy wants to date my mom."

Molly's eyes widen with her smile. "Oh my goodness, he was talking about her the other day."

"Nope." I turn away and cover my ears. "Not doing this. La, la, la."

I drag the mower towards the shop. Molly follows behind me, laughing, poking me in the back. "He said all she needs is a good man. Someone—"

I spin around. "Who's been there. Yes, I know this one."

She covers her mouth, an explosion of laughter leaking through.

"Are you okay?"

Molly holds up a hand, shaking her head, then nodding. I've never heard her belly laugh before and it sounds like she's choking. She flings her hair back and tries to get herself together, but her face is flushed and her dimples are deep and creasing. She grabs her sides, struggling to stay upright. "Just the thought of it. Your little mom and..." She looks back at the garage, bites her lip before she loses it all over again.

"Yuck. You're so gross."

Things are better on the way home. I sneak glances over at Molly, sort of bobbing along to Al Green. I've taken to watching her watch things. The way her eyes scan the streets, the sidewalks, the buildings. Even when we're having a good time, she's poised for danger. Sometimes I go days without noticing where I've been or what I'm doing. For Molly, it's knowing every second.

I turn down the volume. "Okay, so what do you think the girls did today?"

"Hmm, Ana probably drove your mom nuts with questions."

"Or maybe they did face painting."

Molly turns to me, horror in her eyes. I shake my head. "I'm kidding. But since we're talking about painting..."

She takes a breath, throws me a look. "We weren't."

"You're really good. Not that you don't know that, but..." She turns her head, looking out the window. I decide not to push. "Anyway, I'm going to clean out the garage, so, if you want to set up the easel and...do whatever, it's cool."

We pull into the driveway. Molly closes her eyes. "Thanks."

"Yep." She sits there. I sit there. We're both looking at the house. I shift in my seat. "Hey, about Cora, you know, we're not..."

She shakes her head and reaches for the door handle. "Nope. That is a *you* problem."

And with that, she's out of the car, rushing up the path to the house.

17

I find Mom sitting at the kitchen table reading a book to Ana and Ashley. Ashley is into it, eyes rapt, her body perfectly still, while Ana is engulfed in her latest drawing. I'm slightly offended no one leaps up and rushes over to greet us when we walk into the kitchen.

Mom is clear and crisp, remarkably sober. Her roots are growing in and there's some color in her face. Her voice changes with each character, sending me flashbacks of bedtime stories from another lifetime. I hang back, leaning against the doorjamb, until I catch Molly watching me watch them.

"And that is how a fairy finds her dust." Mom closes the book.

Ashley smiles, looking up at her. "Can we read it again?"

Ana's eyes never leave her work. "Hey giant. Look at this one."

She slides the page to one side, and I take a seat at the table, taking in the carnage on the page. It's absolute mayhem. A snake the size of a locomotive thrashes through the metropolis, people hanging onto street posts, buildings, onto cars. Others are not so fortunate.

"Um, wow, this is very...realistic."

"Do you see the legs dangling out of the serpent's mouth?"

I nod. Molly sighs. "Ana, I thought we were going to try to draw mountains."

She wrinkles her nose. "Mountains? Why?"

Molly slides in beside her at the head of the table. "The beach. Sunshine. Rainbows." She tosses her hands up. "Something besides death and dismemberment."

Ana ignores this and points out the finer details to me again. "Look at the bus flipped over, see, you can even see the..."

Molly puffs her cheeks out. "Ana."

Mom gets to her feet. "Well, it is certainly creative." She points to the bus. "Unfortunately, this poor guy is in need of a tourniquet."

I drop my head, hiding a smile. Because again, even with the dismemberment on the page, the house feels real, without the lump of Mom in her bed, the door shut, shades drawn, sleeping off the demons.

Molly gets to her feet and asks Mom what she can do to help. When she does, I spot the pile of bills on the table. Phone. Electric. Water. Something urgent from the city. The city is very urgent with us lately.

Somewhere on the fridge is the school board letter, but before I can worry about it too much, Mom gives Molly a sweet smile and announces we're ordering pizza. This sends the girls into cheers.

LATER, after pizza, I'm out in the garage, tossing stuff around, sifting through the past, deciding what to keep and what to haul to the curb. I start with Dad's chair. Then I slide out boxes, the old ones with my dad's name on them. Ties, shoes, folded button-down shirts, and some self-help books. It's kind of crazy we still have all this stuff, like some sort of time capsule. I'm dragging it all to the curb when Mr. Andrews pulls up in his Audi.

Setting items curbside is a blatant violation of HOA policy, a lesson we found out when Mom set our TVs on the street in an effort to "focus more seriously" on writing.

I straighten as he comes sauntering down the driveway towards me, one hand in his pocket. "Good evening, Nat."

I nod. He's got a blade of grass on his shiny leather shoe. He bends down and flicks it off, looks at the boxes, what's left of my dad's chair. "Hey Nat. You know, trash doesn't run until Monday."

"Thought I'd get a head start." I motion to the box. "Oh, there's some silk ties in here if you need one." I give him my best grin.

He nods to the pile of split leather and wood. "Looks like this chair has seen better days."

"Yeah, had some trouble getting it out."

"Funny," he says in that grim way of his. Time for some chin rubbing, some contemplation here. "Look, Nat. I understand you and your mother are going through some things. Trying to figure stuff out. You've got a lot on your plate with school and..." He pauses here to emphasize the obvious. He knows I slugged a teacher and I've thrown everything away. "I'm also aware that this house is currently, well, that you guys may be having financial issues. But I can't allow this sort of thing to go on. I've gotten several calls about it."

"Yeah?" I say, standing up straight. He's got his arms crossed, probably flexing under his little lavender button down. "What 'sort of thing'?"

"This," he waves at the house. "Well, for one, I saw some new faces the other day. You guys having guests over, or...?"

Or. Definitely or. He looks over to our house, his voice not so soft and caring now. "Because, well, subletting rooms is also a violation of code. Air B's and B's, those type of things. It's strictly prohibited."

"I think it's one word."

"What?"

"No, just, Airbnb. I don't think it's B's *and* B's."

"Well, regardless, I'd..."

"We're not subletting. Hey, do you and my dad still talk?"

He frowns. A slow blink of the eyes. Mr. Andrews, the sensitive guy now. But I'm not having it. If he reaches out and touches my shoulder, I may do something that could seriously hurt my case with the school board. Thankfully, he doesn't. Instead he takes a casual step back. "Nat, I'm trying to help here. I've known you for a long time. Your mother, too. We're more than neighbors, in a way, we're a community, and we need to look out for one another."

I can't help snickering. It sounds like a cheesy political ad. Finished with his oral history lesson, he nods to the boxes. "I'll place a call, get that stuff picked up, maybe have the clothes donated, how's that sound?"

I try to put together some words. I can't. I only stare at the pieces of the chair, to the pile of boxes and books and ties and all the things my dad deemed unimportant enough to leave behind. It stirs up some heat in my chest, but instead of clenching my fists and raging, I set a smirk on my face and look Mr. Andrews straight in the eyes.

"We're not subletting. Just having some friends staying, Mr. A." I look around. "But you know what? If you see any violations around here, you be sure to set your little citations in the mailbox. We'll get them in the morning."

Mr. Andrews gives me his best slow blink, shake of the head. But he's only put off by this for a second. He recovers with the business meeting nod. I smile and shrug, and finally he wishes me a good evening and starts for his house.

1 8

———————

The easel sits unnoticed in the garage for the next few days. Along with the scattered supplies and clothes and empty boxes on the floor with the old toys. Molly hasn't said much else about it, so a few days later, on the way to work, I bring it up again, sort of, clenching my fist, knuckles cracking, absorbing the throb.

"So, I was thinking about Ana, and her uh, drawings."

Molly nods, her gaze set and level. "Oh yeah?"

I tap the wheel. "You think she draws because of you?"

Molly continues to watch the world out her window. I sip my coffee. It's cold and disgusting, but since I don't sleep much anymore, a necessity.

"Maybe," she says, turning to me. "Or maybe she's a sadist with an unhealthy thirst for violent images."

I spit my second sip of coffee all over the steering wheel. Molly's eyes come alive with her smile. "Gross."

"Sorry, wasn't expecting that."

She bites her lip, tucks her hair behind her ear. "So, remember that convention thing you were talking about?"

I wipe up my mess with my hand, glance over to her. "Um, yeah."

Molly's gaze drops, then it's back on me. "Are you still going?"

I shrug. "Haven't really thought about it." A lie, of course. I've thought about it from every angle, and I'm still no closer to deciding. Molly knows it, too. She shakes her head.

"You're a terrible liar."

"A compliment from Molly Martinez. Let me mark the day."

She rolls her eyes. We get to the turn for the shop.

"So, why are you asking?"

Her tightens. She stares at the dashboard like it's a cue card. "Well, um, I was wondering if I could hitch a ride with you."

I hit the brakes, stopping the car halfway in the entrance to the shop. "Really?"

Molly nods. I think back to what her Mom said about trust. Molly picks at something on the seat. "There's a workshop that same weekend. I think it's near your thing. I could give you gas money if you could—"

A workshop. So many questions come to mind. "No, no. I would love some company. But..." I can't stop being surprised by her.

"What?"

"Okay, honestly, I was sort of losing my nerve."

She nods. "I figured. All the more reason I should go. I'll coach you up." She looks back over her shoulder. "Also, um, you might want to park. Half the car is out in the road."

"Right."

I glance over to her, the outgoing Molly, eyes bright, the talkative Molly. The one I never saw at school. "Molly Martinez. Life Coach."

She grabs her thermos and exhales. "Heaven help us all."

We hit the Woodberry campus strong. Since the Fabio thing, I can't help eyeing every car, on the lookout for a low riding Scion. We plow through the hills in the back near the tennis courts, where it's mostly roots and dirt, and then take lunch.

Virg wants pizza, there's a buffet across the street. Molly and I exchange looks. Eating with Virgil is tricky. For one, he talks the entire time, through a mouthful of pasta and pizza crust, chicken parm and breadsticks. And when he's not chewing or talking or spitting while chewing and talking, he's burping, moaning about his acid reflux and how he'll be in the bathroom for the rest of the night.

We take refuge at the salad bar. Virgil prowls the buffet for fresh pizza. Molly picks through the lettuce for the dark pieces while I load up on the carrots. The day is light and hopeful, and I'm feeling the need to mess with her.

"So, you think we'll see your boyfriend today?"

"Only if he's with Cora."

My smile widens. "Okay, I see how it is now."

Molly's laughing, too, but more at me, because at six four, I have to crouch and contort myself to reach under the low hanging glass cover of the salad bar. She moves easily, passing over the onions and moving on to the cherry tomatoes. A fresh pizza arrives, Virgil does a happy dance. He tears into the still steaming pie, taking four pieces, stacking them two deep.

I lean closer to Molly. "You're in for a treat."

She looks over to our table where Virgil spreads a napkin over his gut, singing to himself or maybe the pizza, it's hard to tell. He's sets one fist, roughly the size of a pineapple, on the table. In his other hand is a fork, which he uses to tear into his stack of pepperoni pizza.

Molly frowns. "Dibs on the seat beside him."

Damn. It leaves me across from Virg, in the direct line of fire.

"Okay," Virgil begins, nearly taking down a slice of pizza in one clean swipe of the fork. I watch Molly watch him, a mixture of amazement and disgust as our boss devours the pizza he's stacked like pancakes. He goes in again, the fork coming down, slicing through the layers before he shovels it into his mouth.

Still chewing, he waves the fork between the two of us. "No more games. You paid off them gangbangers yet?"

"They're not..." Molly stops, thinking better of it.

Virgil leans back. "They're not what, gangbangers? Sure as hell looked like it the other day. Now, I should call the police, but..."

Molly looks away.

I sip my water. "We'll take care of it, Virg." Like I know what I'm talking about.

Virg tears back into his pizza stack. "Yeah, sure you will. Let it be known," he says, his voice lowering. The restaurant is full of people, discussing work, sports, life, not...this. Virgil wipes his face. "I'm not onboard with any of this, we clear? So, I don't want to know any details. I lent that money to *you*," he says, pointing his fork at me. "Clear?"

"Yes, sir."

"All right," he says, just as the doors swing open from the kitchen. "I'm going back in. Lots of fresh pie today."

19

It's my fourth trip to Lafayette Estates in a week, and the place isn't growing on me. The mud isn't helping the curb appeal. It's been raining most of the day, which is how Molly and I had time to cash our loaner check and prepare for this little meeting. Molly called Fabio and set things up while I was in the bank. Now she sits beside me, blank as a stone, shut off as we veer down the riddled pathway, sloshing through the puddles and mud.

Molly's face shows little emotion as we slow to a stop in front of the trailer, where, judging by the cars in the driveway and along the yard, there's plenty of company inside. The Cutlass sits there, and I'm tempted to keep going, say we tried and all that. Instead I cut the engine and stop myself from asking Molly if she's okay. Neither of us is okay, but neither of us has a better idea.

A thousand bucks cash weighs heavy in my pocket. Molly looks over to me with a thousand questions in her eyes. I turn to my left, where the redneck trailer sits quietly. The truck is gone, but it doesn't mean I want to hang around and wait.

"Well, this is it," I say, clapping my hands, sounding like an idiot.

Molly shifts in her seat. "I can go in alone, if you want?"

"No, no way." I say it too fast and too high-pitched. It's not that I'm scared, which I am, it's just that, the other day has been stuck in my head day and night. The guy with the cryptic finger guns. Getting beat up I can handle, it wouldn't be the first time. But getting shot is something I'd rather avoid.

We exit the car together. The rain is letting up and a low sun filters through the breaking clouds, shining off the paint of the cars in the driveway, the water beads from sealant and wax. I'm about to make a joke, something corny or awful I'm sure, when the door rattles open and an unfriendly face meets us as we approach the steps.

"Molleee, how are you *chica*?"

Molly mutters something in Spanish as she brushes past him, leaving me standing there, waiting to see if I'm invited to the party. I don't recognize the guy at the door from the other day, as he stares into my eyes, sizing me up and down. Eventually, his face breaks into a smirk. He nods for me to enter. "You brought your bodyguard, no?"

I duck inside where I'm blasted by the sharp smell of weed. My eyes adjust to the darkness, the haze. The room is too cramped and too hot. Four guys lounge on a sectional, legs sprawled on the coffee table where beer bottles and an ashtray sit amongst the trash, wrappers, cigars, and spare change. While the place is sparse on furnishings, a billboard-sized TV spans the wall, blocking a window. Not that there's much of a view.

Fabio sits in a ripped up chair, a king amongst his people. "Well Molly. It's good to see you and your..." he raises an eyebrow. Lots of snorting going on. These guys must think I'm hilarious.

Molly sets her jaw, eyes hardened. Again, I'm thinking, *this* girl, if Molly had set *this* look on Meyers the guy never would have touched her. Finally, she nods at him, as though she's about to spit. "Like I said on the phone. I'm paying you back. That's it. Don't bother me while I'm at work."

I sneak a quick glance at Molly, because the rapid words, the hint of an accent, it's yet another part of her I've never seen. Fabio smiles at me, as if to acknowledge this, before turning back to her. "Aww, come on, Molly girl, stay a while. And look at you two. All-American boy and girl. I like it, really."

Standing there, nothing to do with my hands, or my eyes, just taking up space as they smirk at me, I realize I don't have anything personally against Fabio. This whole living room, the weed—it's nothing I haven't seen before. The only difference is where they're doing it. Last summer, Dustin Miller's parents took off for New Zealand and Dustin threw a month-long party. They pumped the gangster rap, rolled blunts, and emptied the liquor stash in the pool house. After a week or two, the place was trashed. But Dustin's house sits off the hole-six fairway, and he simply hired someone like Molly's mom to clean before Dr. and Mrs. Miller returned home.

Now I'm here with Molly, wondering who, if anyone, is documented, armed, about to go sell weed to a doctor's kid. Another glance at Molly, and once again it hits me: her whole story is nothing short of a miracle.

Molly glances to me and nods, our unrehearsed cue to dole out the cash. I reach for my pocket, thinking for a second it's going to be like the movies and four or five guns will be drawn. Instead they focus on the video game on the screen.

I count it out, take a step, lean over, and hand it to Fabio, trying to hide the shake in my hand. "Thousand bucks, right?"

He takes the money, counts it, then looks up to Molly. "Got you a rich boy, huh?"

I take a breath to calm myself. All the sharp smiles on me. Molly's eyes narrow and she sighs. "Are we done?"

Fabio shrugs. "I'm not holding you hostage." Then, to me. "You are the hero."

"Nope, just trying to be a friend."

He nods. Something in his expression drops, and I see it. It's clear he wishes Molly no harm. But it's gone in a flash, and I'm still itching to get out of there. Molly turns to me and I turn for the door.

"Hey, hero. Treat her well. Those little ones, too. Anything happens to them, well..."

His eyes go wide as he does a cutthroat motion with his hand. I look at Molly, the color draining from my face when they all bust out laughing on the couch. Molly basically shoves me out the door.

We're outside and I'm doing everything but running to the car when we hear Fabio call after us. "Molly."

I nearly trip. Molly whips around, ready to let him have it, when he holds up a hand and motions for us wait. His other hand digs in his pocket and he comes out with a wad of money. "Here, take it. Spend it on the girls."

She stares at the money like he's holding out a dead fish. "No. I owe that to you."

"Nah, you don't owe me anything, Molly. Come on," he says, smiling. Then, looking at me. "She's always been stubborn, you know?" He hands me the money, the bills warm in my hand.

"It's fine." Fabio grins at Molly. "Tell your mama hi." He nods across the street. "I'm glad you're out of here."

Molly nods. Fabio nods. Then we're in the car. I put the key in and drive down the road with thoughts tumbling through my mind.

Once we're up on the main road, Molly sits back and her expression drops. "Well, I guess we can pay Virgil back."

I look over at her, astonished. "What just happened?"

"Or go to Vegas." She nods over her shoulder. "Or buy you a window."

"Molly. What was that?"

She nudges me, a smile breaking through. "I seriously thought you were going to pee your pants."

I look at her closely, her wide eyes, tight lips. It's like she's quaking, bursting at the seams. "Oh, it's funny? I'm sorry, I didn't realize it was funny. I'm glad you see the humor in all of this, I seem to have completely missed it."

And it's then, through the gray clouds and the mist on the windshield, Molly lets it go. Her head shakes and she covers her mouth with her hand. She tries to say she's sorry but can't get the words out because she's cracking up too hard. And then I'm laughing.

Because it's ridiculous, everything, all of this. And while I have no idea what's going on I figure she'll tell me eventually. Besides, when you find yourself stuffing a thousand dollars in your pocket and you're completely, one hundred percent positive it's the last time you will make a mad getaway from a certain trailer park, it's sort of hard not to laugh.

AFTER DINNER, I'm up in my room, phone in hand, scrolling through a post about baby laxatives when there's a tap at the door. Since the door doesn't quite shut (long story), it falls open with a hitch, hanging by the bottom hinge. I look up and see Molly standing there like she didn't know her own strength. I sit up.

Molly shies away. "Oh, sorry, I was just…"

"No, it's fine." I run a hand through my hair, look around, then back to her. "Come in, if you dare, I guess."

She walks in cautiously, her eyes roaming over the room. Piles of clothes, dirty socks, boxer shorts, dishes, are scattered amongst the basketball shoes and work boots and random books and Gatorade bottles. But Molly's not looking at the floor, or my clothes, or at me.

I let out a sigh, acknowledge the holes in the wall with a laugh. "Oh, yeah, those were there when we moved in."

She nods, grabbing her arms at her elbows the way she does when she's shrinking away, getting nervous. It's crazy how this girl can seem big enough to fight off the world at times and seem so small and fragile at others.

I nod my head rhythmically, wishing she'd say something. "So, what's up?"

She turns to me, her dark eyes searching my face like she forgot why she came to my room at all. Then she shakes it off. "Nothing. I mean, well, I wanted to thank you again, for all you've done. But especially today. It was sweet of you. And," she laughs, a nervous chuckle. "I was only kidding earlier."

I set my phone face down. "Oh, about peeing my pants and all?"

She smiles, nods, but again her gaze returns to the holes, the trophies, then to me, and it's uncomfortable. I get to my feet for something to do. People don't come into my room. Cora used to, but no one else since everything went down. So it's weird.

I make a path through the clothes and junk with my feet. I pick up the smallest trophy and blow off the dust. "This was the first one," I say, wiping it off on my shirt. "I was so proud of it. I used to study my name. We were the Sharks, which doesn't make much sense considering the ocean is like two hundred miles away, but I loved it so much, this dumb little trophy. I took it everywhere. See there? Almost wore the name right off the base. I remember my dad kept saying 'See the reward for your hard work?'"

Molly smiles, but it fades quickly. "Was it hard for you, though?"

"What do you mean?"

"I mean, like, basketball. Was it just something you were naturally good at?"

"No way." I shake my head, still staring at the name. *The Sharks.* "I was the shortest kid on the team."

Molly smiles. "Right."

"No, really, I was. Well, wait. I take it back. There was one kid, never came to practice, Walt or Wally something. Damn, I can't remember now."

Molly stares at the trophy in my hand. "But it got easier, right?"

She walks over to my side, looking at the other, bigger, more ornate trophies. The ones from camps and AAU and the Y. She turns back, raising an eyebrow. "I mean, MVP, All Conference..."

"Yeah, I guess. I got my first real growth spurt in the eighth grade. By then I was going to camps and playing travel ball and Dad and Mom were fighting so it was nice to be gone. I don't know if it was basketball or that I wanted to be away."

She keeps glancing at the holes and it's making me jittery. Making me talk just to fill the room. She must think I'm a raging psycho, which I'm not, really, but the holes don't help my case. I try to steer her back, talking more, talking fast—anything to cover it up. "I mean, so yeah, ball got easier, while everything else got worse, but hey, you know, that's just..." I set the trophy back on the shelf, run a hand over my neck.

"Nat?" Again to the wounds in the walls. Each one bigger than the next. She looks down, nods, then tucks her hair back. "It's, it's okay to talk about it, or not. I'm not...you know?"

She's not judging. I get it. But this conversation feels sort of one-sided, and I'm already feeling stupid enough after earlier today. And for, I don't know, talking. I turn to her and roll my eyes. "Kind of a funny thing for you to say, though, right?"

Molly's eyes go hard, like a door slamming shut. "What?"

"Come on, Molly. *Talk?* With you?"

She glances at the door. "Look, I'm sorry."

I shrug. "No, it's fine."

"Nat."

Sometimes I feel myself becoming mean, like it's growing inside me and I have no way to stop it. It's rolling down a hill, heavy and fast and all I can do is get out of its way. Now it's rolling towards Molly. "It's just that, well, it would be nice if for once *you* would talk. Tell me some things, you know?"

"That's not, no. That's not what I meant," she says, shaking me off, taking a step to the door. "Look, sorry I bothered you."

I try to stop myself from chasing her away. "Molly."

"I have told you things. More than..." She sighs, her voice cracks. "I've told you so much."

I walk towards her until I'm facing her, towering over her when she looks away. "You could tell me about painting. Or about Fabio. Maybe just something, anything about you. You're so good at hiding yourself, you never allow anyone in."

She throws her hands out from her sides. Almost panting. Fighting her own meanness from rolling down her own hill. "What do you want me to say, Nat?"

"I don't know. But you come in here, asking me about this and," I stop, look away, swallow it down and try to bring myself back down to earth. "Okay, Molly. What do I want you to say? Hmm, I'll make it easy. You know what I want to know? What makes you happy?"

She stops at the doorway, like she doesn't understand the question. "Seriously?"

"Yeah, come on, let's talk. You're always so...quiet and down. Like, what makes you smile? What makes takes your breath away, brightens your day?" I shrug, wondering what the hell I'm asking her. "What makes you smile, Molly?"

She shakes her head, closes her eyes. "Look, forget it, okay? I don't know what you want from me. But thank you, again. I'm forever indebted."

Always the smartass, I turn away. "You're welcome."

She gets to the door. It starts to close but the hinge catches. "My sisters," she says suddenly. I turn around. Molly's staring at the wall again, clutching herself, forcing her eyes to mine. "Seeing them smile, laugh, giggle. Knowing they're free. Knowing they will always have that here. Knowing they won't have to hide or duck or live in fear. They're here and they can stay. That *makes me happy*, Nat."

Her voice cracks on her last words. I start to open my mouth, but she turns away from the door.

Damn.

20

The smell of bacon wraps me up, setting my stomach in knots. It has me up getting dressed in a hurry, stomping down the steps for the kitchen. The sun slices in through the windows. I'm surprised to find Mom at the stove, fully dressed, jeans and a t-shirt instead of nursing scrubs. Perhaps even more amazing, nothing is on fire.

Ana and Ash sit patiently at the table. Molly is there too, her hair up in a lazy bun. She looks tiny in her oversized sweatshirt and shorts. Just seeing her, and last night—a wave of guilt hits me hard.

She doesn't acknowledge me as I approach Mom, who cranes her neck and gives me a peck on the cheek before I steal a piece of bacon. "So," she says, setting three more strips on the pile. "I was just telling Molly about my plan. I'm taking the girls to the museum today."

I stop before the bacon reaches my mouth. "What?"

The toaster pops and Molly is up. She plates the food, sets it on the table for the munchkins. Ana looks at me with her usual passion for the day. "They have dinosaur eggs there!"

My chest tightens, and my throat threatens to close. "So, like, you're taking the car?"

She nods then shakes the hair from her eyes. "Is that okay? I was thinking I could drop you guys off at the shop."

I glance at Molly who gives me a vague nod. I think about Mom with the girls. Maybe stopping off for a drink. Maybe losing two little girls at a strip mall. I hear the clink of the wine bottle rolling around on the floorboard. I see a fiery car crash, something from Ana's drawings.

I make a fist and suck a deep breath. When I turn around, I find Molly watching me closer. She nods again, more directly, then looks at Mom. "Yeah, sounds great."

No, it doesn't sound great. It sounds like a disaster waiting to happen.

Ana however, is ready to pop. She flings her hair to the side, yammering on about T-rexes and eggs and whatever else she's going to go see. Mom smiles along, bumping me with her shoulder, asking if I would like one or two dinosaur eggs with my breakfast.

Everyone finds it hilarious. Call me a stick in the mud, but considering I've been the only one adulting in this house for the past year, I feel entitled to some caution here. I mean, I'm still adjusting to her making breakfast. It's been maybe four years since my mother has asked me if I wanted eggs.

I lower my voice, trying not to let the girls hear. "Are you sure?"

Mom shoots me a look. "Yes I'm sure," she says loudly, dramatic, offended I should ask such a thing.

I look at the girls. Two pairs of bright brown eyes, munching toast and ready for adventure. I don't have to look at Molly to feel her gaze on me. Finally, I take a breath and nod. "Okay then."

Mom cracks an egg into the bowl. "Well gee, thanks for your permission."

After breakfast, Mrs. Martinez stays at the house with the girls. I drive us to work, Mom in the passenger seat and Molly behind her. "Nat, we'll be fine."

"Yeah, I know. I just, be careful, with the window and all. I really need to get that fixed. Do you have a car seat for Ashley?" I look at Molly in the back, whose eyes are waiting for me.

Mom scoffs. "Did you not hear anything we said in the kitchen? I'm stopping off for one on the way back."

"Okay, but do you know how to put it in? Do you have directions to this place? I think it's off I64, and construction is—"

"Nat." Molly leans up from the back. "It's fine."

If Molly thinks it's fine, it's fine. She's the one who's always sensing danger. I can tell it's different for her though, her worry for the girls compared to the dread for herself or her mother. Maybe to Molly the girls are safe, at least in the eyes of the law, so maybe in Molly's eyes it makes them invincible.

Meanwhile, Mom goes on a tirade about how she wiped my little behind when I was little. She should be able to handle this. It's not her first rodeo, you know. To hear Nat tell it, it's a wonder he survived at all. I'm about to ask if she's come up with any ideas on how to pay property taxes, since she's so productive and all. But I can't force myself to get the words out.

We pull into the lot. It's almost comical how Virg shoots off the trailer when he sees my mom in the car. He swipes at this hair, hustling to us, using one hand to wipe his face and the other to keep his pants from falling.

"How you doing, Mrs. Reams?"

Mom steps out of the car and stretches. I leave the car running and get out and walk around where I stand next to Molly, who basically drags me away to the trailer. I lean closer to her, still in the back of my mind thinking about what happened last night in my room. "He's going to have to fight Gary."

Molly slaps my arm, and I can tell by her smile she's over whatever happened between us last night. We watch Virgil tap dance around my mom. The guy is basically drooling.

I catch a little of what he says, not that I'm trying to hear it. "You got one hell of a kid here. Hang in there. If you need anything at all..."

I turn to Molly. "Hear that, I'm one hell of a kid."

Molly rolls her eyes.

Mom smiles and touches Virgil's arm to convey her thanks before she makes her escape. I watch her get in the car, scoot the seat up and adjust the mirror, my heart clenching as she gets turned around. My little Honda looks a bit more worn putting down the road, leaving me with such worry it nearly folds me over.

Virg is fiddling with something on the truck, doing his happy whistle. Molly's voice is soft. "Nat."

"Shoot. The brake light is out. And the muffler's about to fall off the car."

"Nat, it's fine. You can fix it tonight. Come on."

The day begins with a few residential houses. Sand brick McMansions with lush lawns and enormous garages. We make our way to the offices and businesses before we hit the hills. We finish early, drenched and heaving as we find a spot in the shade to wait for Virg, who's still out with the Hustler.

Dark, silvery clouds roll over the horizon. The wind picks up, playing with a strand of Molly's hair. Sitting here, we're hidden from traffic by the hedge of holly bushes that poke my arms bloody when I have to trim them. Molly sits against a tree, legs pulled up, watching the sky. I'm in the freshly cut grass, our diagonal tracks meshed like art.

I squeeze my fists, enjoying the wind and trying not to worry about the brakes on the Honda or Mom driving in the rain. I wipe my forehead. The silence is different between Molly and I now. Comfortable, settling, like a bridge of trust.

After a few minutes I shift my body to face her, nudge her foot with mine. "So, the first hole in the wall, the smallest? I was fourteen. Freshman basketball game. I fouled out and we lost in overtime."

She turns to me fast, recovers, lips parting then closing. She sets her cheek against her knee. I sweep a hand over the grass clippings, working to get the words out—words I've never said to anyone before.

"I remember this new kind of rage forming, like a strength

surging through me. Not so much because we lost, but," I shake my head and smile. "My dad had walked out in the fourth quarter, phone stuck to his ear. I guess I should've been happy he even came, he worked out of town a lot. But I was at the free throw line when he took a call. He stood, and I remember dribbling, then stopping, then watching him walk out. The door shutting. The ball hardly hit the rim."

Molly's eyes stay with me. I take a second then go on, laughing for no reason at all. "I made the second free throw, though, made two more later on to send the game into overtime before I fouled out." I shake my head. "But he never saw it, he never came back in the gym. When I got home, Mom made all these excuses for him—work is stressful, it's a big account and everything—but I could tell she was pissed, too. I got out of the car, slammed the door. I thought I was over it, thought it was gone, that rage. I told myself I didn't care. But the anger kept building, kept rushing into my chest, and by the time I got to my room it was like, I felt like someone else. My book bag slid off my shoulder and I zeroed in on the wall."

I turn my head to wipe my eyes. "My fist went straight through the drywall, pieces crumbling, falling on the floor. Lucky I missed a stud, right?"

"Yeah," Molly whispers.

I nod. The wind picks up. The rain inevitable now. We should probably head for the little gazebo thing near the road, but I feel like if I stop now, I'll never tell her, maybe never tell anyone. I make a fist, study my knuckles. "Okay, so the second time was after Dad moved out. Like, I came home and all his crap was all over the place. Mom had halfway checked out by then, so she was no help. I mean, I'd heard them fighting—like, every night, but something about the way it went down, how he left while I was at school, you know? How sorry is that?"

My eyes are beginning to burn. Molly lifts her head, wipes her forehead, then sets her chin on her knees. "I'm sorry, Nat."

I shake it off, seeing the wall, feeling it on my knuckles. The crumbles of my anger on the floor, under my feet. "Well, this time I took a trophy, slung it at the wall, the base of it hit and stuck. I ripped it out and bashed it in there again. You wouldn't think it would feel as good as a fist, but it got the job done."

The grumble of a diesel truck slows, the swish of breaks and the squeak of the trailer—the sounds I've come to associate with Virg. Through the bushes I see a blur of red. "Well," I get to my feet as a few fat drops of rain hit, "looks like he's just in time."

Molly gets her mower. And as we drag them to the curb, she calls out to me. "What about the third one? Weren't there three holes?"

I almost stop, because she still wants to know more. I look at her just as Virg stops the truck. I let down the gate. "Let's just say Mr. Meyers wasn't the only thing I hit that day."

Virg does the talking on the way home. The rain hits hard and the wipers struggle to keep up. "Got done just in time. They said storms at three and it's three on the dot, how you like that? They finally got it right."

I think he's still flying high from this morning. I nod along through his jokes, but I'm stuck in the past, still thinking about Mom and still hoping she's being safe, hoping the window isn't leaking. I turn to look out the back when Molly's hand knocks against mine. I shift again, and she takes my hand and gives it a squeeze.

It's the tiniest thing in the world and yet it sends a flood of heat through my chest. Virgil talks about how we can spend the rest of the day sharpening blades and cleaning equipment. I look over at Molly, her eyes bring me in. She doesn't say anything but she doesn't have to. I nod.

Virgil runs into the gas station for another gut buster soda. He forgets his wallet and runs back to the truck cursing and grumbling and sopping wet. We let out a little gush of a laugh. It's good to be moving on to something else. A present worry instead of an old one. I lean closer to Molly. "You think Mom's back with the girls by now?"

She shoots me a look. The first crack in her armor. "Why don't you call her?"

I pull out my phone. Molly and I are still sitting arm to arm even though Virgil is in the store and she's no longer cramped against me. Mom's phone goes to voicemail. I look at Molly and shrug. I could say I told you so but I don't. I ask Virgil to give us a ride to my house.

I don't want to be right about this.

21

Virgil grumbles about giving us a ride home. He doesn't like it one bit, he tells us, how we're not going back to the shop. He'll have to unload the trailer then clean up everything. He goes on for a while, but I can tell it's mostly an act. I think he's secretly stoked about possibly having two chance encounters with my mom on the same day.

I would be enjoying it more—watching him paw at his hair, check himself out in the mirror at stop lights, wipe down his oil stained shirt, and work to get the sunflower shells out of his beard—if I wasn't so preoccupied. Spilling my guts to Molly and now wondering about my mom with the girls has left me with no desire for small talk.

Again, Molly finds my hand, and we're not quite holding hands, just touching, but I don't dare move.

Coming down the street, my stomach sinks because the Honda isn't in the driveway. The rain is tapering off but the sky is still rumbling. Virgil takes a deep, deflated breath. You want me to hang around, or...?"

"No, we should be fine," I say, opening the door. Molly slides out and Virgil gives me this look, this greasy grin I can't bear to look at. It's clear he thinks we're just trying to be alone at the house.

"All righty, see you kids tomorrow. Be care—"

I shut the door in his face.

Virg gets the truck backed out. Molly and I take to the garage, looking out at the empty driveway. The easel sits there like a question. Molly starts for inside but stops at the door.

"Nat?"

I stop pacing. "Yeah?"

"She's fine. Okay? It's fine. So please stop freaking me out."

"Yeah, sorry."

I look at my phone, willing it to ring. The door shuts and Molly is gone. My head is all over the place, first with the confession, then I'm worried sick about my mom, and yet still I can't stop thinking about Molly's hand against mine. It's bad timing, all of it, and I don't want to get hung up on this girl I'm trying to help. This girl who doesn't trust. Who won't let me know her. This girl who is helping me.

I'm on my feet when Molly comes back to the garage in her customary tank and shorts, her hair down. She starts to pace, walking on her toes, but stops herself, playing with her hair tie. "Mom's at work. Did you call again?"

"Huh? No. I just..."

I look at my phone.

"Nat, I know you worry about your mom. But I can tell by the way she looks at the girls she'd never let anything happen to them."

The rain comes back, steady, even as the clouds collide and part. I want to say, *Maybe not intentionally,* but I let it pass. Molly walks over to the easel, runs her hand over it. Minutes go by and Molly stares at the easel like it holds a painting only she can see. I wait, only the sound of the rain to go with our thoughts. And then...

"Okay, my turn. So, art class, eighth grade. My teacher, Miss Manual, said I had talent." She looks at me, her eyes sharp. "Talent. No one had ever noticed me before, much less thought I was *talented.*"

This is the Molly I enjoy the most, the confident one. The one with bright eyes and an easy smile. The one who likes to tease and joke. Again, she stares at the easel, an old friend, her eyes floating with the memory. "Anyway, she entered one of my paintings into a show and it got honorable mention. I was horrified, because, well, you know, my little secret. Miss Manual had no idea, of course, so she didn't know why I was hyperventilating at the sink."

"Did you tell her?"

Molly turns to me, her eyes searching mine like I'm missing something important. "I've never told anyone, Nat."

She stares at the easel, and I'm left shaking my head at the secrets sitting between us in the garage with all the mess and comfortable silence, when the Honda comes cruising down the street.

Rain or not, the radio blares through the open windows. Mom and the girls singing Brittany Spears' *Ooh Baby, Baby* at the top of their lungs.

Molly closes her eyes with her smile. I start to rush out but knock my head on a snow shovel hanging from the rafters. The car stops and Mom, wearing sunglasses in the rain, gives me this big, gorgeous wave. Ashley, able to unbuckle herself, comes tumbling out from the backseat, leaving Ana to scream for someone to help her with the seatbelt.

"Moooooollly! Giant!"

Molly kneels. Ashley comes crashing into her. She's soaking wet and without a care. "Oh my gosh. You should have seen it."

"Did you see dinosaur eggs?"

"Uh huh," she says, eyes wide, breaths heaving. She's sort of rabid, her head shaking compulsively. She's got something blue at the corners of her mouth. "They had these huuuge skeletons. And we got to watch a movie there, and then we got to build our own skeleton!"

Mom and Ana come up behind her. Ana is holding Mom's hand and looks a little sleepy. I smile. "You guys had a good time?"

Mom nods, stifling a yawn. "Oh yeah. Sorry we're so late getting back. My phone died."

"No problem," I say, glancing at Molly. We all head inside. Ashley is still bouncing around. Molly takes Ana's hand and looks back at me and smiles.

Mom yawns, shakes her head. "They wore me right out."

And that's it. She heads up the stairs to go down for a nap.

Later, after the house falls quiet, Molly comes into the kitchen where I'm making a sandwich.

"So, they're both out cold. I only had to read two stories instead of the usual six."

I smile. "Are you hungry? Someone actually went grocery shopping."

Molly shakes her head then steals a piece of turkey. "So, are we still going to the thing this weekend?"

"Oh yeah. That."

She bites her bottom lip and nods. She's being weird, her breath kind of shaky. Me too, I guess, now that I'm thinking about it. "I don't know about my thing anymore. I mean, what's the point, right?"

Molly nods, shoulders slumped. I fold the sandwich together. "But I'm still giving you a ride, though. So, what is this workshop anyway?"

She looks up. "Huh? Oh, it's a legal resource class. For undocumented, um," she clears her throat. "Undocumented students." She gets it the second time, says it like it's no big deal. "But I mean, if you're not...you know, only if you're already going."

"Wait, what? Molly. For real?"

She takes a breath, her hands fiddling at her waist. I try to downplay it, but I'm floored. "No, it's great, really. And um, I'm not sure if you've noticed, but I really don't have much else going on. Yeah, let's do it."

She closes her eyes, digs her toe into the floor. "I'll give you gas money."

"Did we get paid today?"

"Some, we haven't exactly been working a whole lot."

"No, but we've got a thousand bucks to blow, so..."

"Shouldn't we give that back?"

I look at my sandwich. The counter shines. The whole house shines. "I suppose. Hey, are you okay?"

She eyes the floor, stares at her tiny feet. She rocks back a bit and nods slightly, like some confirmation to herself. She takes a big breath and says, "I want to tell you about Mr. Meyers."

I set my sandwich down. Her gaze is locked on her feet. It feels like the air has been sucked from my lungs. She waits for me to recover. I look at my hands, then to her. "Molly, you don't have to."

She blinks a few times, shakes her head. "He kept finding reasons to keep me late, to have me stay back and help. Whenever I did, he'd ask me questions. I think you know how much I hate questions. Anyway, these questions kept getting more and more personal, inappropriate, if you know what I mean."

Her voice is hushed, wet, scraping with pain. "I'd ignore him but it didn't matter. He would start squeezing my shoulders. I'd ask him to stop and he'd laugh, say I needed to relax."

She shakes her head. When she looks up at me, her eyes are wet and glossy. "He wouldn't stop. He said he could help me. He said he knew, you know, my 'situation'." She groans as she says it, and I can't believe she's telling me this, in this quiet house, ticking with normal sounds, safe with our families' sleeping breaths.

Molly picks something from her shorts. "I quit staying back, almost quit chem altogether. Then one day, *that* day, he said it was super important. About my grade and all. He needed to talk to me. And this time I said yes. Because I wanted to talk. I wanted to tell him he wouldn't touch me again or I was going to the principal. I mean, I wouldn't, but that's what I planned to say. But when I did, when I finally said it. He laughed in my face."

She looks right into my eyes. "He laughed. Then he started kissing my neck, telling me to 'relax, just relax.' That's about where you came in."

She keeps looking at me, like she's checking to see if I'm blaming her or judging her. I'm not. I'm thinking what I could have done differently. And now, with her talking more and more, it feels like I should try to make her feel better. But all that comes out is, "I'm so glad I punched that dude."

Molly snort-laughs through her tears. She wipes her eyes and smiles. "Yeah. Me too."

22

———

It's still dark outside my window when my phone starts chirping. I roll over and see that it's four thirty in the morning, then turn back over to ignore the intrusion. Wait. My eyes snap open and I'm wide awake. Because it's Saturday. And we're driving to D.C. today.

The still-chirping phone shows three texts from Molly, each more aggressive than the last.

Good morning!

Wake up already!!

OMG Get up!!!

Don't make me come up there!!!!

I have an endless supply of exclamation marks!!!!!

A t-shirt won't cut it. I'm going to be in the same town as my dad and Kristen—even if I'm not going. Probably not going. Still, a sudden jolt of nervous energy hits and I change into a button down, blue shorts, New Balance sneakers without socks.

Only then it looks like I'm trying too hard. So I go back to the t-shirt, run a hand through my hair, which has now curled at the ears, and gently nudge open Mom's door. I pad over to find her in the dark, lean down and kiss her warm forehead. She lets out a snore and that's it.

It's all worked out. Mrs. Martinez has a rare Saturday night off. Mom has been mostly sober this week. Things should be fine. But...

I know how *should be* or *could be* works out. I *should be* or *could be* in school this fall.

The looking ahead to an adventure was great. The planning with Molly was exciting. The actual getting in the car and driving up the road to D.C. ignites a clawing in my chest. But before the worry and dread can bury my will and pull me back up the stairs to my bed, there's Molly in the kitchen.

Her silhouette burns against the light over the counters. Her backpack rests at her feet and she's clutching a bottle of water. As hard as this is for me, it must be a million times harder for her. Yet, when she looks up and sees me, she grabs her backpack, loops her arms in the straps, and says, "I have Nutragrain bars and bananas. Should we take cereal?"

I smile. Sniff the air. "Did you make coffee?"

Molly scrunches up her nose. "I did," she says, handing me a mug. "Now come on."

We get moving, racing the approaching dawn, hurrying to the car before the day catches up with us and sheds light on what we're trying to do. It's peaceful at this hour. The neighborhood is still tucked in, and the air is cool and wet with dew. Molly plops into the Honda and sets her book bag between her feet. I can't imagine what she's brought. Notepads? Books? A change of clothes? I search her face in the dark. She's focused, determined, strong. Clearly terrified.

"Everything okay?"

She nods several times, talking herself into it. I crank the old beast and put it in reverse. And so our journey begins.

On the expressway, Molly shifts and digs into her bag. I sip my coffee. She's a mess, coming undone with every dash in the road, flopping back, again with the foot tapping. She stares out the window towards the hint of sunrise. Her eyes fall to her lap. She twists and squirms.

"Molly?"

"Yeah?"

"Seriously, are you okay?"

She turns to me but her eyes don't make the trip. "I've never left them. Not like this."

"Ash and Ana?"

She nods.

"It's just for the day. Everything will be fine. Remember, like last time with my mom?"

"This feels different."

"We'll be home tonight."

She bites her lip, nods. There isn't much traffic, a few headlights behind me. It's five thirty-eight and the sky is a grayish blue. Molly leans over, checking my speed, checking our gas. Checking everything. Because as close as we've become, it's still easy for me to forget her life is one big obstacle course.

Eventually she peels a banana and takes a bite. I fiddle with the radio and find an oldies station. Otis Redding's *Sittin on the Dock of the Bay* hums to life. I bob my head. Molly raises her eyebrows.

I bob a little harder, anything to make her laugh. I snap my fingers and shoot her a look. "What? It's a good song."

"Okay."

"No, what?"

"Nothing. Just, I mean, is that really how you dance?"

I change it up some, fingers drumming on the steering wheel, rolling my shoulders. "What? What are you trying to say?"

She shakes her head and eats. The song turns to static, I hit scan on the radio. "Whatever. I'm a great dancer. And you should hear me sing."

"I have, even over the mowers. I think we're safer with the dancing."

"Okay, show me what you've got then."

"Um, no," she deadpans.

I snap my fingers. "You know you want to dance. What sort of music do you like, anyway? I don't even know."

She looks at me, then back to the window, then back to me. I shrug. "Come on, I know you like Al Green, right? Mom's got some other stuff in here, in the visor above your head."

"Well, I like country music."

I turn to her. "No. Please say you're kidding. You are kidding, right?" Wow, I think she's blushing. "Seriously?"

Molly squints at me. "Oh, I'm sorry, was I supposed to say mariachi music?"

"No, I..." I look out the windshield, then back to her. "That's not what I meant."

She looks down to her lap. The song ends and some other old song cranks up. She flips the visor down, looks to me with a smile, and laughs. "Nat. I'm messing with you."

"Oh."

Molly fiddles with her ponytail, pulls it tight then lets it go. She shakes her head. "You're too easy sometimes."

Up ahead the sunrise charges into the sky, pink and red and bleeding through the clouds. I drive straight for it, at least until the interstate where the traffic picks up with commuters.

I change the dial on the radio. "I can try to find a country station if you want."

She starts giggling. It's a beautiful giggle, like a child, the way she loses herself for a few breaths, gasps then grabs her sides and tries to reel it back in. I'm so glad I got to know it, know her, because most people have never heard Molly Martinez giggle and that's just a shame. Soon I'm laughing too.

"You know what, you're getting Reverend Green." I hit the CD button and the drums roll in as *I can't get next to you* plows into the speakers.

Things calm down in the car. Down the road I turn to her again. "So you've never spent a day away from your sisters? How could you be so cool the other day when they went to the museum?"

She looks over to me, eyes heavy with a smile. "Because you were a wreck."

"Huh. I really had no idea you were so slick."

She sits back, her eyes taking in the road, the horizon. "But no, I've never left them. I mean, the other day, I got to see them off, you know? But *I've* never left home, really. I walk them to and home from school. To the park. Everywhere."

"Wow. What did you tell your mom?"

She exhales, sets her head back, and closes her eyes. "She thinks I'm wasting my time. She doesn't trust lawyers, she says I'm going to get myself arrested. But I'm not, this is just as important for her as it is for me."

I nod, like this is some casual conversation After all this time we've spent together, it's still weird to think we're doing this. Part of me enjoys it, how Molly's comfortable talking about this with me. My old friends and I talked about going to Cancun, crossing borders, and partying. We never once worried about freedom or rights or police. College was assumed. Same for cars, clothes, success in general. But another part of me is still stunned. I mean, *this* is what is important to Molly. Basics.

I glance over to her again. "So, what do you want to study? In school?"

Without hesitation she turns to me. "I want to go into child development. Teaching."

"Yeah?" I say, nodding. "I can see it."

"I mean, this workshop. It's *something*, you know. Otherwise, my whole life will just be, I don't know, waiting. Does that make sense?"

"Yeah," I say, because waiting I can relate to. "It makes a lot of sense. Like with my mom. I come home, make sure she's okay, but I never feel like I'm moving forward. And now with this board hearing, I mean, yeah. Waiting."

She nods, sets the banana peel in a grocery bag she brought for trash and takes a huge breath. "You know, today, hopefully there will be people who can help with applying to college."

It's almost a whisper, like college is a dream, a birthday wish not to be uttered out loud. I start to say something, to remind her she makes straight A's and college shouldn't be in question. But sometimes Molly just needs to talk without me talking over her. Besides, our roads are so different, even when we're on the same path, like right now. Here I'm headed to a swanky hotel conference center, Molly is going to a workshop for undocumented students.

She sighs, looking out at the cars on the road. "I might, I mean, there's a chance I could even get financial aid, grants, scholarships, even though I have no social security number. I never knew this could happen. And now, well, at least there's hope, right?"

I drive, unsure how to respond. Hope. Dreams. A pursuit of happiness. An honor student—despite the distractions, disruptions, the constant threat of upheaval—determined to better herself. So she risks everything to find that hope, that dream. She's hoping to find hope. And even that causes her guilt.

Again, I can't think of anything to say, and yet I see no reason to turn the stereo up. So we drive for miles without saying another word, within the growl of the Honda, the flutter of the plastic bag in the window, barreling down the same path towards our biggest fears.

2 3

In Northern Virginia, the traffic squeezes in around us. The lights take longer, the driving more stop and go—which doesn't do my brakes any favors. We pass one string of shopping outlets and hit the next, thrown to a grind of four lane traffic, work trucks, commuters, vans, pickups, motorcycles, and some seriously brave bicyclists.

At the red lights, I watch Molly take it in, the girl who's never been anywhere. I watch her tense and startle and shrink into herself. The day has gotten warm and I set the windows down, stuffing the trash bag window under the seat. The Honda seems like it's aged a few more years during the trip. I keep an eye on the climbing temperature gauge. A little less than half a tank of gas, but I pull into Sheetz to top it off and so we can get snacks.

"I have snacks." Molly holds up her book bag.

I hold up my empty coffee mug. "Yeah, but I need more caffeine."

I park and she starts to get out but the door handle sticks, and so I hop out and rush over to her side, making a show of getting the door. "Madam."

Molly looks down to the door handle. "Such a gentleman."

The place is packed with people pumping gas, getting breakfast, getting on with their morning routines. I grab two biscuits and a coffee, offer one to Molly who shakes her head. I try not to notice her eyes shooting around, looking for trouble. But where I used to joke and try to get her to talk, now the whole situation just makes me mad.

Back in the car she relaxes. But not me, not for the first time it occurs to me how Molly dresses, the way she fixes her hair and never wears jewelry or even earrings. I take in her maroon t-shirt and khaki shorts, how she keeps herself as plain as possible, so she never draws attention. And my anger only builds, watching this amazing girl—someone our school should be parading around as a model for middle school kids—tuck herself in and hide from the world.

I pull out of Sheetz and we get about one hundred feet before a red light. I squeeze the steering wheel, but then shake it off. Because we're going to try, we're both driving up here to at least try and do something about our lives.

I turn to Molly. "Have you ever driven a car?" She squints at me. I shrug. "I'm just curious."

"Actually, yes. I have driven a car once."

"Yeah?"

She smiles. "I used to sit on my dad's lap. He'd do the gas and brakes and I'd steer. Does that count?"

I squint my eyes in mock deliberation. "Hmm."

"I drive better than you," she says, nodding ahead. "You've almost rear ended ten cars now. And you pulled out of there like you were trying to kill somebody."

I turn to her, ignoring that last part. "What? I am a cautious driver."

"You hardly pay attention. You're too busy fixing your hair, or, are we still calling it *dancing*?"

"I'm not *fixing* my hair," I tell her, throwing it back. "This doesn't need fixing."

Molly busts out laughing. "Yeah, okay."

We hit a light and I make a show of braking early, leaving three car lengths ahead. Molly rolls her eyes and calls me impossible. But

I'm still hung up on things. I try to frame my question delicately, but it's easier just to ask. "So, I mean, can you apply for a license?"

She cuts her eyes to me, then shakes her head. "Nope. At least not in Virginia."

I tap on the wheel, taking this in. "Well, you could live up here. Take the metro."

I'm determined not to sit here and stew. I can't spend this whole trip feeling sorry for Molly Martinez. She doesn't want that. It's why she answers me the way she does, short and quick, her voice light and dismissive, ready to move on.

Eventually, we go back to the silence. We drive without talking. A few forever-long stoplights and I'm fiddling with the radio when Molly turns to me. "My dad had a truck. It was registered in a friend's name. A Ford, he loved it so much, used to wash it every Saturday," she says with a laugh, "even though it had all these dents and rust spots."

"So what happened to it?"

She looks at me like I'm crazy. As though whatever happened, her dad's truck was the least of her concerns. "I don't know."

I get back to the radio, for something to do. Maybe to dance and try to make her laugh. But when I go to put the reverend on Molly smacks my hand away. "Okay, Al Green is great and all but we need something else to listen to."

"Be my guest. I was just about to start singing, though."

"I think you should go," she says, handing me Mom's Mazzy Star CD. I raise my brow, shrug, then set the CD in the player. The drifting strums of *Fade into You* set me back into my seat.

I wouldn't be making this trip, considering a possible face-to-face with my dad, if it weren't for her. And I no longer sit around feeling sorry for myself and about what happened since Molly and her family moved in. I'm inspired, for the first time in a long time.

But I can't show her, so I look around like a smartass. "Go where? I'm driving."

She doesn't laugh. "You know what I mean. Go see them. Go get some answers."

MOLLY WORKS MY PHONE. She instructs me on the exits to take, which lanes to be in. Besides the directions, things have gotten quiet in the car, the closer we get the more we fidget. I can't tell if she's anxious or excited or both like me. From what she told me earlier, she's attending two or three workshops. The first is titled, *Know Your Rights*, hosted by an ACLU lawyer. *Know your rights*, I repeat it in my head. Even after my own fall from grace, it's humbling. Never once did I consider *my rights*. It was like oxygen. Just there.

It takes us nearly forty minutes to navigate traffic past the leafy trees and over a few bridges to a much more industrial setting. We find the building. We're running late as we pull down Canton Street. Molly is fumbling with her bag, zipping, tightening, her hands a whirl of activity as we pull up. It's on the back end of Milton Row, a low slung, dirty beige building. It's a crappy place to go searching for hope. It looks about as inspiring as a day at the DMV.

I peek to my right, Molly is quaking with energy.

"Do you want me to come in?" I say, watching the people milling around the door. I catch bits of Spanish, some staggered English, pieces of other languages. Everyone is brown or black and they all share the same weary gaze of desperation in their eyes.

Molly shakes off her nerves and brushes a strand of hair from her face. "What? We just talked about this. Go to your thing."

A quick shrug. "I told you, I'm not going."

She manages a grin. "Sure you are."

I look away from her, to the people lining up to find hope. Molly dips her head to meet my eyes. "Look, we both have goals today. And we are both going to meet our goals before we go home."

I nod. "Wow. You really do sound like a teacher." Molly scolds me with her eyes. I squirm. "So I just barge into this...whatever the hell it is and stroll up to my dad. Kristen. What then?"

She lowers her head. "Improvise."

"Improvise. That's your advice?"

"Yeah, I don't know. Tell your dad you came to see him. Give him a hug."

"What? No. I'm not hugging my dad."

She shrugs. "You want to see him. If you didn't, we wouldn't be here. This was kind of your thing before it was mine, remember?"

"Yeah but..."

She's got all her stuff in her lap as she turns to me. "I've got to go. Now you go."

Out the windshield the white sky still holds a pinkish tint. "I'll be back at three. Right at three, okay?"

"Mmm hmm." Her eyes float over to the people, the traffic, the vendors setting up for the day. I've never seen her so nervous.

"You okay?"

She takes a quick breath, nodding, finally meeting my eyes. "This place is crawling with lawyers. If I'm not safe here, well, there's really no hope at all, is there?"

It's a big question, one I can't answer. We say goodbye, and again she tries the door, and again it sticks. It must be broken now, and so I leap into action, which means nearly getting creamed by a moving truck.

Molly eyes me like a crazy person as I open her door. She steps out with her bag, brushes her hair out of the way. "Well, thanks."

"Call me if anything comes up. I'm just like, you know..." I turn, as traffic whizzes by. "I'll be somewhere nearby, I think."

She laughs, an honest, nervous laugh. "Okay, three. All right?"

I nod. She starts for the building and I watch her walk down the sidewalk, getting smaller and smaller until she turns, opens the door, and enters the building.

2 4

The truth is I didn't have to punch Mr. Meyers.

In those first seconds after I ripped him off Molly, he turned to me, furious, wild, and for a second his face settled into the usual pretentious way he regarded me in class. And somewhere—if I'm still being truthful—maybe it wasn't only protecting Molly that led to him lying on the floor, hands at his face, his nose leaking blood on the tile.

Afterwards, I stood there, hulking over him, somewhat aware of that silent promise I'd made. Molly had already run off by then. And as it began to settle in, what I'd done, I scooped up my research papers—spattered with Mr. Meyers' blood—and set them on his desk before scurrying out to the hallway.

I left my chemistry teacher in the other room, crumpled, writhing around, moaning, kicking his feet into the shelves. An hour later I sat in Principal Vicks' office, staring at my research paper on her desk, sealed in a plastic zip lock bag, like some ghastly piece of evidence in a murder case.

Meyers wasn't in the office or at the school. Mrs. Vicks sat rigid behind her desk, clutching her phone in case I lunged for her, explaining to me how poor Meyers was at Woodberry Memorial Hospital. He would have to take medical leave, because I'd assaulted him. Assault. I was too busy rolling my eyes to say much.

She said he likely wasn't going to press legal charges, which he certainly could, she wanted me to understand. She seemed to be studying me. I should consider myself lucky for that, she said. I couldn't go around using my size to bully people—teachers or anyone else. I could have injured him much worse.

I sat in the chair, blanking out as she recited the school's zero tolerance policy. She already had my transcript at the ready and quickly pointed out how my grades had plummeted in the past year. Did I have anything to say for myself?

By the time I thought about explaining what had really happened, I thought back to Molly, the sheer horror on her face in those seconds afterwards. The slight shake of the head, the whisper in her voice as she pleaded, begging, just before she ran off. So that left me in the office with Mrs. Vicks. And as she stared me down, waiting for what I had to say, I wasn't sure why, but I couldn't bring myself to do it.

So I had nothing. Nothing when she shook her head in disappointment. Nothing when she suspended me for the rest of the year. Nothing when the school board sent mandatory expulsion papers to my house. Nothing but my own arrogance. Because back then, I assumed it would all blow over. I'd watched my dad get out of speeding tickets, find loopholes when he did his taxes. I'm from Fenwick, and kids from Fenwick Estates didn't get expelled. They didn't get charged for weed or underage drinking. Things just kind of worked themselves out.

But things haven't worked out.

And if that wasn't enough, I learned the rest a few weeks later, near the end of the school year, when I ended up at Molly's door—my very first trip to the lovely Lafayette Estates. But my words left me when Molly's face went pale and the terror came over her all over again. I held my arms up, assuring her I wanted no trouble. This was before I knew anything about her, and I thought she'd be itching to tell her side of the story. I needed her to do that.

So I got her the job, or a shot, as Virg called it. I explained it to her as I took in the chipped concrete stoop, the muddy yard, and the torn screens, the shredded vinyl siding. The confederate flag across the street. And then I left. Molly never said much of anything. But she showed up for work the next day.

Virgil made her cut the hills and shovel mulch out of the truck and do all the grunt work. But she kept coming back and never complained and he said she could stay. A few times I approached her about Meyers, but it was clear she wasn't going to talk about it. And the more Molly showed up and refused to talk, the more it sunk in: I was completely alone in this.

And I'm alone as I pull up to the Mosely Convention Center, ten blocks and several galaxies away from the immigration center. A sea of gleaming SUV's and high-end imports line the parking lot as I wedge my exhausted Honda between two shiny Cadillac Escalades. I turn the key and stare out the windshield.

Ten percent battery as I check the schedule on my phone, then the blog. The convention is filled with seminars, workshops, speaking engagements, and the all mighty endorsements. Seems Kristen is still "over the moon" about the product placement symposium. It's her favorite phrase, over the moon. She really needs an editor.

I squeeze a fist and realize my hand is no longer tender. The knuckles are normal size again. I take a sip of too sweet/too cold coffee, grab my backpack, and step out of the car. No need in locking it, considering the back window. With a shrug, I toss the keys on the floorboard. It's more likely to get towed than stolen.

I take my time approaching. The place is huge. Old but modern, brick but updated, with well-groomed courtyards, dog tail grass and ornamental trees. Traffic and tourists mill about, but it's a parade of baby strollers that tells me I'm in the right place. Bags and bottles, kids strapped to chests. Yep, this is it. But I'm losing my nerve.

It was easy giving Molly a pep talk, but what am I really doing?

The only thing pushing me is that I told her I'd go. And she went. She marched right on into her building, even as what she's doing is a lot more dangerous. I have no worries about getting stopped and asked if I'm supposed to be here. Worst case scenario they turn me away and that's it.

There's no one checking the door, and besides, there's too many people. The lobby is super sleek and huge. The swirly carpet makes me dizzy just looking at it. It's chaos. Bright white smiles, gym toned arms, fake tans, lapels and placards with dangling ID tags. People at tables peddling self-help books, working mom products and how-to's and all the latest trends.

I try to hang back and blend in but my height makes it impossible. A smiley woman calls out to me. "Young man?"

So much for that. A lady with a gray ponytail waves me over to a table. I swallow and make my way. "Hi, are you listed?"

I don't know what she means. "Oh, I'm looking for my dad."

"I see," she says, every wrinkle deepening as she regards me like a lost puppy dog. "Well, what's his name, I'll check the log."

I look around. "Um, Dan Reams, I think he's here with Kristen Reams."

A quick look back to the double doors, as though saying his name will summon him. The first layer of sweat hits my back just thinking about my dad strolling out to the lobby with his super blogger wife and some little kid. But it's too late.

"Okay," the smiley woman says, plugging away at the keyboard. Around me is a whirl of conversation, polite hellos, explosions of laughter. Lots of arm touching and hugging going on, compliments abound. Women, a few men too—with babies bouncing on hips, rocked back and forth in strollers, some crying, squealing and fussing —chat with each other. Freebies are dished out. Dannon, Dove, Aveto, all have kiosks and tables. *Here, take one, no take two!*

I'm trying to hold it together for this lady at the counter, still half expecting Kristen and Dan to appear from behind a curtain. The lady nods, her bangs bouncing with the trip. "Okay, yes. Here it is.

Kristen and family." She points to another counter. "You can just head over to check-in and they'll take care of you."

I give her a weary smile. "Thanks."

"Okay sweetie, good luck."

I get moving. I force myself not to think about how much harder that might have been for someone like Molly. But I'm almost obsessed with it now. *Someone like Molly.* Someone undocumented. Someone not...white? Privileged? Confident? My whole life I've flashed a smile and assumed it was the same for everyone else.

Now, peeling back the layers of wealth, class, and race, I have all sorts of questions. And as I find my way around babies and bodies, the first question is, what had I envisioned by coming here? I start down a hall and take a left, avoiding the check-in station. I pull on one of the double doors and it clanks open. People turn to look. I've entered a workshop full of women holding babies to their breasts. They all turn to me, adjusting and scowling.

"Um, I, uh..." I quickly shuffle back and get moving. Really, it's only a matter of time before security hauls me out of here.

Back in the lobby I manage to find a schedule. Kristen is speaking in the McGhee Room at eleven. It's nine right now, and I'm already hyperventilating.

Although part of me wants to skip the school board hearing altogether, grab my GED and head to community college for night classes, I can't convince myself to let Meyers get away with it.

Last year, some rumors spread about him getting touchy-feely with the girls. Nothing concrete, more like a running joke in the hallways or at parties. Meyers is maybe thirty or so, he likes to think of himself as super hip and witty. I've stalked his Facebook, clicked through his skiing pics, his posts, one of him playing guitar. A real laid-back guy, tan and barefoot dude, he likes to brew his own beer and go to shows. From what I'd heard, he'd hung out with Emma Casey and Katie Riggins at a festival. He'd told them to call him Scott. Emma said he'd gotten wasted and invited them back to his camp. They didn't go, but it always stuck in my head. Dude is a slime ball.

Where does that leave me? Do I show up and face the board, break my promise and explain myself, describe in detail what I saw and let the board decide my fate? Maybe I could talk myself into it. But again, what about Molly?

Before it happened, Molly was a face in the crowd, a girl who never said much, kept her head down and took notes in class and never spoke to anyone. But now, knowing what she's holding—her secrets, her family, her many talents—it's something I want to protect. And the promise. I can't ask her to testify on my behalf.

Would they really deport her? On the news all I see is the gang members and drug dealers. But Molly? I can't see deporting a Cum Laude hopeful, shipping her off because she wasn't born here. What about Ana and Ashley? They're American citizens.

It's confusing. And as I find a seat at a window, hiding in plain sight within the chaos, I go the other route. One where I don't explain myself to the board. I take what's coming and get my GED, go to community college, then maybe walk-on a basketball team. The path gets trickier, windier, carrying all that baggage. But I know Garner High too well. I'm stuck with the baggage either way.

In the distance sits the Washington Monument. A bitter laugh escapes as I shake my head, thinking how Molly finally made her field trip. She's across the bridge, fighting for her life. And as I gaze out to the point pressed against the morning horizon, I'm inspired. Because it makes me want to fight too.

Maybe not the school board, but I need to confront my dad, because he shouldn't be able to go through the rest of his life without facing what he's left behind.

With all this renewed energy, I march towards the main conference room, swing for the doors and scan the room for a place to sit and get myself together. Again, there's like twenty round tables, people spread out, two to three at a table, and every one of the heads turns to look at the guy at the double doors, making all the noise.

At least the lady up front doesn't call me out. I find a place at a back table where only one other person is sitting, checking emails on a laptop. I have no intention of actually listening to any of this stuff, probably pushing some sponsorship dribble anyway. Just need a minute to pull my thoughts together, figure out what I'll say to old Dan. Looking around, I don't see him in the room. I take a seat as the speaker discusses mental balance and parenting.

Two percent battery. I glance up from my phone, to the presenter. Typical power point behind her as she delves into the impact of a parent's mental health on a child. The presenter's voice is deep yet soft, confident, as she discusses how mental health issues pose biological risks as well as psychosocial. Another glance around. No Dan. No Kristen.

I walked in to zone out, try to get myself together. But the more I hear, the more I can't help leaning forward, hanging on her every word.

"While mental health is not contagious, studies have shown a genetic link. Not only that, there can be traumatic effects from the exposure to behavior associated with mental illness."

She's fit, in a business jacket, skirt, eyeglasses. Her short, light brown hair falls to her shoulders. Her voice is in command of the room as she starts in on risk factors. I rub my arms, my face, chilled from the air conditioning but also because it's a little weird, her choice of words. It's almost like she's talking to me directly about Mom.

This lady is certainly hitting every box on the checklist: poverty, marital difficulties, single parenting, unemployment, substance abuse, poor communication, and so on.

I check my phone again, praying it won't die. Dr. Margaret Wills, PhD. Her blog is full of info (useful info, links and studies and statistics), and I can't help but notice it doesn't have one sponsor listed or contest or giveaway or *place your banner here* alert. This will take further research. I save it to my favorites.

Up front, the screen flips to a graph. Dr. Wills delves into the child: self-esteem issues, coping skills, problems at school. My neck prickles. I glance around, looking to see if everyone else finds this as fascinating as I do. I find a water on the table. A muffin too. I'm taking mental notes, hanging on to keywords. Things I can try with Mom. Ideas on how to engage her, try to talk to her.

A woman at our table sneaks a peek at me, maybe because I'm fidgeting, or because I keep making a fist, grimacing, moving my lips with my thoughts. It's become a habit, the squeezing, the familiar throb of pain, almost something I'm unaware of. I make myself stop, give her a smile. She turns away.

Dr. Wills paces the small stage, and for the first time in a while, I feel like maybe I'm not the only one with a mom who sleeps twenty hours a day, who has all but given up on everything. Even with the recent strides she's made—with Ana and Ash being at the house—I live each day waiting for her to fall back into her hole.

Dr. Wills finishes up to light applause. I pocket my phone, now drained to a brick, as she takes questions from the front I can't quite hear. Snagging another muffin, I make a clumsy escape to the lobby, ducking out and shoving through the big double doors and making all sorts of noise again.

Outside the conference room, I squeeze my eyes shut, catch my runaway breath, and attempt to calm down. Strangely, it's not anxiety hitting, but something different, something hopeful, and that's a whole lot scarier. I dig my charger out from my bag, find an outlet and plug in. Then, still feeling bold, I take a seat on the ledge and call DeShaun.

I don't even know why DeShaun. But I tap his name and the phone is ringing.

Moms swoosh past me, speed-walking in both directions, laughing, gushing about beets and baby laxatives. DeShaun picks up, sounding groggy. "Natty, what's up?"

I haven't heard his voice in a while. "D, hey man, how are you?"

"Good, good," he says with a yawn. "What, you don't sleep anymore?"

It's only ten, but it feels like a day has passed since Molly and I jumped in the car and pounced on dawn. "Hey, I need to talk to you, got a minute?"

Another yawn. "Okay, yeah."

Between the road trip and Molly's thing, this thing I'm doing—whatever it is—it's easy to forget that these are urgent matters to us and only us, not to people trying to sleep in on a Saturday. I clear my throat. "So, my hearing is Tuesday, you know, with the school board?"

Silence in my ear. I look around, all the smiling faces. I think about everything Dr. Margaret Wills said, but it was different in there, it made sense, like I was under some sort of spell. Now though, the spell fades, replaced by a familiar dread. It's heavy, creeping up my feet, to my legs, my chest. "I uh, I was hoping you guys would show up, the team. I mean, I guess Coach can't come, but I was..."

More silence. I hear some rustling on DeShaun's end. It's funny how my mind builds these things up, like a sitcom or movie, where the team bands together as one and demands a change. I shut my eyes, grab the back of my neck and shake my head. "Forget it, I shouldn't..."

"Nat."

"Yeah?"

"You never told me what happened. Never told any of us, you know? I mean, everyone at school knows Meyers is a creep, but I mean, you attacked a teacher, dude. Why?"

Why? Hmm. And that's the problem. People need a reason to jump on board. I take a deep breath. DeShaun takes a deep breath. In games, when we weren't playing the way we should be playing, it was always DeShaun, more than coach, really, who took us in. Always even, never rattled. Always smooth. We looked to him and he would nod and clap and tell us to play our game. Now he's asking me why. "What were we supposed to think, Nat?"

My back finds the brick wall. I bury my head down, elbows on my knees. My eyes burn and it feels like I'm falling into a cave. "Hang on." I set the phone out from my ear, set my eyes in my palms, because it's nearly impossible to dig out of this hole. "Okay," is all I can say. When it is not okay at all.

I'd put so much into my research paper. Stayed up for nights working on it because I wanted to fix my grades. Not just for basketball, I wanted to prove to Meyers that I was more than a dumb jock. I remember the quiet in the halls, the distant squeaks from the gym, the few random clicks or coughs, but otherwise just my feet sliding on the smooth floors, the rows and rows of lockers. Then, opening the door to Meyers' lab, the quiet struggle in the back.

Eventually, I set the phone to my ear. I tell Deshaun. Tell him the whole thing, leaving out Molly's name because I don't want her involved, even though she is involved—she's the victim in this whole thing, not me. Wow. It might be the first time I've truly realized as much.

DeShaun listens as I go through the details. He cuts in occasionally to ask a question or have me repeat a few parts. When I'm done, after I've told him about the blood and the blackout and the research paper and the meeting with Mrs. Vicks, I take a deep breath and wait. And Dr. Wills was right about one thing, maybe communication is a good way to feel better about something. I feel like I've unloaded a houseful of weight.

After what seems like forever, DeShaun exhales. "Damn, Nat."

"Yeah."

"Are you serious? You've been sitting on this?"

I can tell he's on his feet now. No more yawning. I picture him rubbing his face, that splotchy goatee he's been trying to grow in. "Yeah."

"Who was it? Who's the girl?"

"I can't say."

"Why? Why haven't you said anything? To Vicks or guidance. To Coach, man?"

Another breath. I run a hand through my hair. "I don't know. For her, I guess, that's part of it, but after a while, it just became, I don't know, what happened. It was just what happened, you know?"

"Uh uh, nope. I mean, this is your life, Nat. You had like, three colleges interested in you last year." *Had.* He catches himself. "I mean, you know. Might still. You still set on Woodberry?"

"Yep."

More silence. I jump as the doors open from the conference room. I sit up as the hall fills. I keep an eye out for Dr. Wills.

In my ear, DeShaun takes a breath, probably pacing his small room. He has two sisters and a brother and things are cramped for a guy pushing six five. "Well, this girl, she needs to come forward, I mean, #*Metoo* and all that, right? What if all this is true and Meyers has been doing this for a while? It needs to come out."

It's weird. Everything he's saying is exactly how I felt until I met Molly. I swallow it down. "Oh, I'm pretty sure it's not the first time for Meyers. But the girl, she can't do this, D. Really, she can't come forward."

DeShaun scoffs. "Why not?"

"I don't want to say. I just need you guys, okay?"

"Yeah, yeah. Look dude, I'm glad you called me. I wish you'd done it sooner. Let me talk to everyone. I can't say for them, but I'll be there, okay, Nat? Text me the details."

"Thanks, DeShaun."

"Where are you anyway? It sounds busy."

"You wouldn't believe me if I told you."

He laughs. "Okay, man. Just...be good, all right, Nat?"

I end the call as another conference lets out, and suddenly it's madness all over again. I unplug my phone and grab my bag as the doors shut. Then, because apparently I'm going to spend this entire day surprising myself, I enter the empty room, banging through the doors for the third time.

Two Latina ladies work furiously to clean the tables. I think of Mrs. Martinez and every individual story in this city. Some glances come my way, but then back to cleaning.

A few women have hung back, talking with Dr. Wills. She must be something, I listened to her speak for fifteen minutes and went outside and called DeShaun. Like she'd cast a spell on me. I still don't know what I'm doing, but I know I can't leave until I speak with her.

I find a table up front that's already been cleaned. A vacuum cranks up near the back. I think I'm being sneaky, trying to appear busy on my phone when she looks at me, nodding her head at the woman talking her head off, but catching my eye. She's around Mom's age. She has a warm, pleasant sort of face. She's all put together, yet approachable.

When the ladies make their way, she does it again, locks me in. I get to my feet and well, I have nothing.

"Hi there," she says. And as much as my feet want to leave, I feel like a stray cat being coaxed out of a corner. She walks over to my table and asks if she can sit down.

The doctor caps her bottle of water and opens her mouth to say something when a sheepish fangirl makes her move. The girl moves in, slowly, clutching a book. She's tiny, maybe late twenties. Her hair is died a bluish gray.

"Um, I'm sorry," the girl says to me, like I'm someone. With stars in her eyes, she sets the book out with both hands. "Um, hi, Dr. Wills? Your book sort of changed my life. I was hoping you would sign it for me?"

Dr. Wills smiles, pats her shirt pocket but the girl is ready with a pen. I look at this lady, her name tag reads "Rose" in small block letters.

Dr. Wills opens to the first page. I sit like a mute watching Rose fill with joy as Margaret scribbles inside her book. She closes it and hands it back to the star-struck woman.

"Thank you so much. You're so amazing."

Dr. Wills' smile broadens. It looks sincere. "Thank you for coming, Rose," she nods at the book. "And for reading my book."

Poor Rose looks like she just might faint. She nods at the doctor, at me, I guess thinking I must be related to or work for the great Dr. Wills. Then she starts off, looking back once again before she retreats.

When she's gone, Dr. Wills looks at me. "Okay, that doesn't happen very often."

I smile. "I don't have a book for you to sign."

She shrugs. "Yeah, well, I'll set up my table later, $15.99. My signature comes free of charge."

We introduce ourselves. And, the way she talks to me, like we're old friends, it slips my guard and puts me at ease. I look around the room, at the massive amounts of food. The fruit is quickly inspected for imperfections, bananas and apples replaced and tossed. The cleaning staff hustles, bagging trash before setting off to go clean something else. Again, I can't help noticing they're all brown or black.

Dr. Wills tilts her head. "I saw you back there, are you with your parents, or...?"

I shake my head. "No, um." I run both hands through my hair. "I don't know."

She sets a chin in her hand, like what I've mumbled is a perfectly acceptable answer. Despite my shakiness, it's comforting, the nice, easy-going way she has about her. It's like nothing gets to her. But I don't get why she's so interested. I try to deflect. "So, you're like a shrink?"

"Among other things. I used to practice law. Now I'm reformed. I teach. And do this," she says, arms up, taking in the room.

"Oh, uh, wow," I say, realizing I'm not exactly utilizing the English language to the fullest, but I'm a little out of my league here. I'm sort of freaking out, too.

Dr. Wills shifts, smiles. "But I'm still enough of a shrink to have noticed you back there. The only one listening. Well, you and Rose, I guess."

I go for a banana sitting in a bowl with apples and oranges. It's perfectly yellow and firm. Thinking of bananas reminds me of Molly and her backpack. I hope she's finding what she needs today. I hope she's doing better than I am right now.

Dr. Wills waits me out. With nothing to lose, I might as well talk. "Okay, so what you were saying earlier, about mental health. It was almost like you were describing my mom. I mean, *really*, describing her. It was kind of weird. I guess that's why I came back."

Again, she waits, her blue/gray eyes sinking into me, patient, relaxed but with a hint of concern. I look away but keep talking, keep blabbing, telling this nice lady—this total stranger—about my life, my issues, my fears. The past year. Mostly about Mom, some about Dad.

The more I talk the more confusing it sounds, start and go and stammering until it's like someone else has taken it over, someone unpacking a string of crappy luck, fate, consequences, or whatever it may be. Next thing I know, I'm going into detail about Molly and her sisters, only how Mom seems to be doing better around Ana and Ashley. I smile just thinking about them, the little fairies. Still, I continue, sputtering along, we're in a ton of debt and I'm not sure where to go next because I may get expelled but now I've called DeShaun, which has me confused, like I'm scared to be happy about it.

"Sorry, it's a mess. I just..." I stare at the table. "I needed to say it out loud."

She reaches out for my hand and everything screams for me to pull away, but I don't. I blink. "Nat," she says softly. "I won't sit here and tell you I have all the answers. I think you know I don't. But let's start with school, the expulsion. You said this teacher was inappropriate with a female student?"

I take my hand back, clench my teeth. I don't want to talk about Meyers, but Mom. I shift in my chair, wipe a hand through my hair. "I just, why does all this fall on me? Why does my mom get to live in make believe, you know? I never get to ask those questions. I'm about to be expelled from school. No more basketball. No scholarship, but she's out there in her own world. Ugh, I just..."

A low, guttural sound leaves my throat. I wipe my eyes but my whole face is wet with tears. This is ridiculous.

"I want to help you, Nat. If it's okay?"

That's when this woman—this speaker, author, lawyer, doctor—pulls out a pad from her bag. She asks where I live, my name, my number and address. I rub my eyes, yank at my hair. But then again, what can it hurt?

She jots it down, then her eyes are back on me, in my eyes. "Nat. Listen to me. Let's get your mother the help she needs."

"We don't have insurance."

"You're what, sixteen, seventeen?"

"Seventeen. Yeah."

"You don't need to worry about that. Okay?"

I laugh but it's a hiss. The sound of someone between sobs. "Why? Why do you care?"

The door opens. A group of women sweep through the doors, all wearing little dresses and belts, jackets and boots, clicking and jingling as they storm the stage. I straighten my back, turn away and wipe my face. They move chairs and set up tables, adjust the mic stands and screens. They look at us and mouth "Oh" like they're interrupting something.

Dr. Will smiles at me and nods. "We can make this work."

I shake my head, ask her again. "Why do you want to help me?"

She blinks her eyes slowly. "Because I had a son once, Nat."

I'm not sure what she means. But the room gets busy fast, shuffling and laughing and it isn't long before Dr. Wills is getting noticed again. I gather my things, sling my bag over one shoulder, and I'm reaching for an orange when Kristen walks in.

She's twenty feet away. Blonde and smiling and going on about the wireless mics. I go blank on the spot. My mouth dries to dust as the room tilts one way then recovers. Another door to my left swings open and some IT guys take over the stage.

Kristen reaches out and touches the wrist of another lady, gushing about how Casey is napping with her daddy. It's so cute, she says, they've had a big day, and she's not so sure they're going to make it through the whole weekend, she says, clutching her very pregnant belly. Laughter, depreciating eye rolls. I know I should stop staring at her but I can't.

She's pretty, I guess, in a manufactured sort of way. And she's shorter than I guessed. I mean, it's sort of hard to judge a person's height by stalking them online. And maybe that's why it's so weird seeing her in the flesh. I've only seen her as pixels on a screen, an internet world away. Now, here she is, the woman who sleeps with my father, eats dinner with him, talks money and makes plans with him.

I jump when Dr. Wills pats my hand, reeling me in. She stands and hands over her card and information. "Call me when you get home, okay Nat? And if you need me before then, I'll be here. I'm really glad I met you, okay?"

I recover, nodding at her then the card. I'm about to thank Dr. Wills for listening to me when Kristen rolls up and introduces herself. "Hi, I'm Kristen Reams. Welcome to Building Your Brand."

It happens so suddenly I don't have time to panic. She smiles and tells Dr. Wills she's a big fan, her blonde bangs bouncing with her movement. I'm thinking she must spend a fortune on hair products, then again, they're probably free.

I wait for her to look at me and know. To recognize my face, maybe from a picture or through its resemblance to my father's. I brace for impact as Kristen sweeps a hand around the room, smiling, talking fast, nodding and waving to anyone who happens to pass. And she's going on about the lighting when I realize Kristen is only concerned with things pertaining to Kristen.

So I'm safe. Or am I? Didn't I want to confront them? Wasn't that the point? I look down to find Dr. Wills' card trembling in my hand, and it's clear I can't do this. I can't meet them. I can't face my dad. What would it prove, anyway?

I need to leave. Now. I turn and start to walk, but my wobbly legs feel like they do after an all-day tournament. I'm only steps into my escape when Kristen says, "Excuse me?"

She smiles, her straight teeth bleached to an ultra-white shine.

She throws her hair back and says, "I didn't mean to run you off. Are you not staying for my presentation?"

I glance at Dr. Wills, look back to the door. "I uh, well, I need to use the restroom."

That's when Kristen squints at me, like you would if you weren't sure about something. And I'm waiting for the question. *Have we met before?*

My throat closes. I cinch my bag, shuffling. Dr. Wills starts to introduce me. "This is Nat. Nat Re—"

"Hi, nice to meet you," I say, cutting Dr. Wills off before she can say my last name. Kristen's last name. Kristen shakes my hand, her eyes already roaming the room to the women pouring in, filling tables. Her attention fleeting, I manage to scrape together some words. "No, uh, yes, I'm coming back, I just have to head out and..." I start backtracking. Dr. Wills watches me closely, surely diagnosing me with seven sorts of disorders as I fumble through my exit. "Yeah, uh, just have to..."

I crash into two nice ladies clutching swag bags and giggling. Smiling like an idiot, I bow, then get the hell out of there.

I find the last stall in the bathroom, lock the door and set my head in my hands. I stare at the marble floors until they blur and bend together, interrupted only when someone shuffles in with a cough and takes a urinal just outside my stall. And maybe this is rock bottom, hiding out in a bathroom so not to face my dad's girlfriend while a man grunts and huffs and struggles to conjure up a piss. I'm hardly breathing. It gets to the point I'm thinking he might pass out, when he finally gets a dribble going. Mr. Andrews comes to mind. *Not bad for a guy in his forties.*

How could I think it would be so easy to waltz in here, introduce myself and...then what? Suddenly it seems like an incredibly stupid idea. And there have been some gems. Like punching a teacher, to name one.

Why do I care, anyway? Dan Reams is not my dad anymore. One more makes four, not five, as far as they're concerned.

The urinal flushes. The man hocks up something into the sink on his way out. I sit back, look up at the ceiling. Talking to Dr. Wills has me off my game. The way she looked at me, like she knew what I was feeling, I don't know. She seemed like someone who knew there was a way out of this.

I check my phone. Nothing from Molly. Two texts from Cora, reminding me I'm a joke. Maybe it's the physical distance between us, or maybe it's something else. But Cora isn't worth the worry anymore.

I send a text to DeShaun with the date and time of my hearing. If anything has come out of this trip, it was calling him.

I get to my feet. I've had enough of the Mommy blogger conference. If there's an answer to my housing situation up here, it's not going to be solved by Dan Reams.

With my head clear, I return to the land of the living. The panic recedes, my chest loosens up, and my breath comes easier. Without the weight of my worry I hit up the lobby for food. I find a chicken salad sandwich, apple juice, and another orange in case Molly wants it. I'm basically stuffing my bag when two security guards come marching over.

"Hey guys." I shoot them a smirk. Because it's a freaking Mommy Blogger conference, not the Democratic Convention. I bite into an apple, content to see how things will play out.

The taller of the two straightens himself, nearly standing on his tip toes. It happens a lot, especially with older guys, like they can't stand some young punk being so much taller than they are. He gives me a once over, solemn and serious, his voice crisp, all business. He's a guy with aspirations of shedding that polyester jacket.

"Do you have credentials, sir?"

Another bite. "I'm sort of on a school field trip."

"Sort of?" He exchanges looks with the more slacker looking officer. This one has a splotch of mustard on his shirt and can't seem to help himself from checking out all the MILFs in the lobby. After a moment of deliberation, Mr. Serious concludes I am, in fact, being a smartass. He goes for his radio, proving he means business.

He barks something to the effect of, *A-23 at lobby, may need a BSR for an A-23.* He's looking awfully smug as he holsters his radio.

He motions for the revolving doors. "I'm going to need you to step outside with me."

I chomp into the apple, chew, and shrug. We turn for the door when I hear a voice I recognize. "Gentlemen, is there a problem?"

Dr. Margaret Wills, clutching a shoulder bag, book, her confident tone gaining control of the room. She blinks twice. Mommies everywhere stop and gawk, looking up from phones and whispering as a joyous hush comes over the lobby.

Mr. Serious eyeballs Slacker, who gives the doctor a full once-over and smiles in approval. "We were just checking for this gentleman's pass."

Dr. Wills shakes them off with a wave of her hand, a magic wand, that thing. "Oh, no need for that. He's with me."

They look at each other again, and I may or may not be grinning like a jerk. Mr. Serious goes for the radio, then decides maybe the matter is not worth pursuing. He removes his hand from my elbow. "Okay, no problem. Thanks, Dr. Wills."

Slacker nods and smiles, and then they turn and go the other way. I look at Dr. Wills. "I could have taken them."

She cocks an eyebrow. "I don't know. Did you see the size of his radio?"

I laugh, adjusting my book bag full of contraband. Dr. Wills nods at the door. "Come on. Let's go for a walk."

I offer to take her bag, since I'm sort of like her assistant now. She smiles, hands it over, and we exit the well air-conditioned lobby for the baking hot sidewalk. The sharp smell of the tar melting off the street rolls over us with each gust of taxies and buses, Fed Ex trucks, vendors, and vans, we start down the block, the edges of the sidewalk black with rubber from all the curbside tires.

The doctor casually says, "So that was her? Kristen?"

I take a breath, think about sitting in the bathroom stall, hiding out. I look over my shoulder, up at the conference center, then to her with a nod.

Dr. Wills looks down to her feet as we walk. I laugh because she's rocking some Nike Air Max's. It's like, all business suit then, BAM, sneakers. I take in the sounds of the city, the revs of engines, the hiss of brakes. We round the corner where a guy plays the drums on some five-gallon plastic buckets. He's smiling, eyes closed, face to the sun, like there's no place he'd rather be than beating on those buckets.

I stop walking. The beat of the drums ricochets off the office buildings. "I sort of stalk her blog. It's how I knew about this," I wave my hand. "This whole thing."

She doesn't raise an eyebrow, doesn't miss a step. "So, she doesn't know you?"

I shake my head. "Nope. I guess not. I doubt my dad's even mentioned me." It sounds pouty, but I can't stop myself, stop telling her things. Maybe because I'm out of town, maybe because she's a doctor and I'll probably never see her again, but it's nice to exhale and let it go. To complain and be petty. "Guess he's too busy with his real kid."

As we walk, I give her the rest of the story, continuing the Nat Reams confession tour, picking up with the *One More Makes Four!* blog. And I still don't get much expression on the doctor's end, at least she doesn't show much. Although I do catch her eyeing my fist and I unclench it. I drop my hand and smile.

She nods to a ledge under a tree and we sit. And again, since I'm hours away from home, and feeling inspired, terrified, bold, with everything in my head firing off at once, I tell her about Molly. Really tell her. I tell her about Molly's status, what happened at school, how she's across the bridge, and I'm so happy yet scared for her.

Saying it out loud—this great life-changing plan of ours—it all sounds so naive. But when I tell Dr. Wills that, looking off, up to the gleam of the office buildings, she takes a breath. "Everything is life-changing, Nat."

"Yeah, I suppose." I look down at my shoes where the toe is starting to split at the seam. I'm going to be wearing fourteens soon if my feet don't stop growing.

"What time you wake up or leave your house can change your

drive. What you wear can affect your mood. Who we meet, well, that can easily alter our course—our lives."

I shoot her a look, realizing I'm probably blushing. "I know this sounds corny, but, it's like Molly and I have been thrown together or something. And that's the other thing. Now I don't even want her to come to my hearing with the school board, because, I mean, she could get deported, can you believe that shit? Oh, sorry."

She waves me off. "A straight-A student? No, we can do some things, there."

We. I leap off the ledge. "Really?"

She nods. "Well, it won't be easy. But her story needs publicity. People need to know a student like Molly is at risk. But most of all, she needs a lawyer."

I think about our thousand bucks. A retainer. I start pacing, trying to get my mind and body to cooperate. How she said something could be done for Molly, just like that, it has me rattled.

"You said your father is in there. Do you still want to see him?"

I'm torn between fixing my life and fixing Molly's. I can hardly breathe and talk at the same time. But Dad? That's not going to fix anything. "Um, no. Not now. I mean what's the use, right?" I nod back, over my shoulder. "He's got *that* life. It might be better for me to stop stalking mommy blogs, you know?"

She chuckles, and I wonder if it's a bad sign that a real shrink is laughing at me. Her phone rings for maybe the tenth time and again she looks at it, makes a face, and ignores it. I try again to sit but I'm too worked up, besides, my brain functions better when I'm moving. "You probably have all sorts of things to do, right?"

"Well, my speaking engagement has been fulfilled." She looks off, then to me, motions for me to sit. "Look, let me make some calls. See what we can do, okay?"

I take my place on the ledge again, my foot jackhammering away. "What we can do?"

"Yes, try to get your mom some help. Perhaps, we can do something about your school hearing. For this friend of yours, Molly, too. Let's get you moving ahead with changing your life, Nat. Wasn't that the point of you coming here?"

"Yes, but..." I'm so used to bad news I don't know how to process what she's saying. The esteemed Dr. Wills leans her head over to get my attention.

"In the meantime, I have one job for you to do."

"Yeah, what's that?"

She turns to face me head on, no longer with the hint of a smile, her easygoing way. She looks directly into my eyes. "You are not to lose hope, got it?"

I nod. She shakes her head as though it's not good enough. "Am I clear?"

I smile, a real smile. I even sort of mean it when I say, "Don't lose hope. Got it."

2 8

———

Traffic is heavy on the way to the immigration center. It's heavy everywhere. And while I'm early and in no hurry (the Honda doesn't respond well to hurrying), my heart thumps with urgency. There's so much to tell Molly, I don't want to forget any of it. And so I weave, get lost, backtrack, get lost a second time, think about life-changing stoplights, and end up on a one-way road behind a row of warehouses. I eventually find the street, where I park and hustle down the sidewalk, buoyed by my newfound hope and Dr. Wills and everything that happened at the *Her Turn* conference.

I clench and unclench my fists out of habit. For the past year, "tomorrow" has been this vast, black void in my head—a wasteland of nothing. And now, maybe, I have something to replace the void. Not sure what it is yet, but it feels lighter.

I'm so engulfed in my own thoughts that it isn't until I'm in the lobby that I notice all the attention on me. It's clear I have crossed through one world and into a new one. One without corporate sponsorship, swag bags, free facials, and stroller reviews. The beige floors are worn to the bone, the smooth, cinderblock walls are plastered with corkboards filled with flyers and attorney phone numbers. Where I was only moments ago surrounded by peppy, blonde, ultra-white smiles from mommies taking selfies and comparing resorts, I'm now amongst people whose faces grip a silent fear that won't let go.

My height, skin color, the way I walk in, screams without words. Where I've just hurried down two blocks without even looking at my surroundings, I'm not sure anyone else in this room has ever once felt that luxury.

It's a grind in here. All silence and suspicion. I nod to the lady behind the counter and make my way down the hallway to the sparsely filled classrooms. I find one with an open door, walk in with my head down, and take a seat in the back.

The teacher speaks in rapid Spanish. She pauses briefly, casting a lingering eye on me. Nope, this is not the Hyatt.

Still looking at me, she says plainly, "I want to speak to my lawyer."

A dry swallow, I turn left then right, wondering why she's telling me this before the classroom repeats it back in a chorus of accents, tones, desperation. A chill runs down my arms. The speaker's gaze stays on me. The eyes aren't angry or afraid but level. I find a handout on the desk beside me. The text is in Spanish with English subtitles, a how-to guide about dealing with immigration agents, reading warrants, emergency planning checklists.

Again, I'm in a different America. One with flickering lights and rattling fans. One where the branding is not so lavish.

I'm thinking about rolling out when a woman near me raises her hand. In broken English she explains she's worried about the raids. Are they becoming more common? Is it true what people are saying, what she's seeing on the news? The census, volunteers, the citizenship questions. Stuff I've never given a second of thought about.

The lady reminds me of Molly's mother, not because she's Latino, but because of the terror sitting beneath her eyes, the tremble in her voice. It's identical.

The instructor nods, alternating between languages. "Yes, maybe. It could be where things are going. Political currents come and go, but the important thing is to know your rights—that you do have rights. Your children have rights. If nothing more, that's what I want you to take home today."

She instructs the lady not so sign anything before speaking to an attorney. Never let ICE in the house. All I'm thinking about is Molly and her mother. How her sisters were born in America but little good their citizenship will do them without their family. How Molly's mother only goes to work, never near a school, a courtroom, or any government offices. How completely alone and isolated she must feel.

I look over the handouts. I listen to question after question all confirming a fear I've never had to face. Of worries I've never encountered. Sure, Mom and I have our share of issues, big issues, but basic human rights is not one of them.

The session ends. I exit with my head down, walking quietly out into the hallway. I look for Molly, peeking in another room, but it's full and I'm not so sure I want to go barging in again. I hang on to my pamphlet, in case Molly doesn't have this one, and head outside to wait.

I find a bench, pull out my phone, swipe my fingers, and press. Kristen's mommy blog pops up. But then I stop, close out the browser. Because why? I'm done stalking her blog. It's pointless. I hope she and her kids have a nice life with Dan.

Instead, I look over the info Dr. Wills gave me. A listing for an attorney who does pro bono work. A doctor in a town thirty minutes away. If I can convince Mom to talk to a lawyer, then go to a doctor, maybe some weekly meetings, in whatever order it takes, who knows. Maybe she can get well, find a job. Maybe we can figure out what to do with the house. It's a lot to want. I'm stressing out just thinking about it.

I'm leaning against a brick wall, staring at nothing, when Molly walks out. She's got a stack of papers against her chest and her book bag is stuffed to the gills. She flips the hair from her face, looks left, right, then her eyes light up when she sees me.

"You're here."

I get to my feet, hold out my arms. "I'm here."

I don't know why, but I walk up to her and give her a hug. And she hugs me back, tightly, both arms as people walk by and notice us, the tiny Latina girl and the tall lanky white guy. Or maybe they don't, but I feel her stiffen, and I let go.

"Sorry, I just. I..."

She waves me off, shaking her head. Then, still on her toes she looks me in the eye, kind of pulls me in then shoves me off. "So, tell me all about it."

I shake my head. "You first."

She sets her face to the sky, wipes back her bangs, and her face gives way to the biggest smile I've ever seen. "It's just hard to believe, Nat. It's like, maybe there's hope."

Chills flush down my arms. It's exactly how I feel. We're the two most hopeful people in the world right now. At least on this sidewalk, outside the plain brick building, surrounded by strangers. We're so full of hope we might drift away.

The chicken salad sandwich I snagged from the hotel is smushed and looks like bird poop, so we spring for lunch at a diner on the next block. Molly's all for it, because this day we are not the Nat and Molly from work. We're not the downtrodden landscapers who dream about the campus they groom. We aren't even two kids from Woodberry. We're life-changers, dreamers, we're two kids ready to take control of our lives.

We take a back booth at the window where the foot traffic sweeps past. Horns and bells and bikes and buses. For once Molly hardly seems to notice as she talks a mile a minute about the workshops. I interrupt with snippets of things Dr. Wills said. About not seeing my dad and why it no longer matters.

She's flipping through a handout from a workshop. I tell her about the one I found. What the instructor was teaching. Her eyes go atomic.

"Wait, hang on. You went into a class?"

"Yeah, why? Is that bad?"

She shakes her head. "No, I just, I mean, wow Nat."

"Yeah, I was all jacked up from my thing and sort of barged in. I was looking for you, and I just took a seat. Molly, I can't, I've been living with my own problems, but, I had no idea..."

Molly shakes her head and takes a deep breath. "So you've had a busy day. I'm sorry you didn't see your dad. But you saw Kristen. Holy shit, right?"

I lean back. "Did you just curse?"

She nods, smiles. "I think so, yeah. How'd I do?"

I'm laughing too hard to answer. We look out the window, catch our breath. "Yeah, so I saw Kristen. It was pretty much what I expected. But then, my dad, right?" I'm about to tell her about how he was up in the hotel room, but, why? I shrug. "I think I realized it's not worth it, you know? If he wanted to see me, it would have happened a long time ago."

Molly's gaze falls to the table. "Maybe."

Our food arrives, and things get quiet. Until Molly's eyes light up again. "Oh yeah, wait." She starts digging in her book bag. I smell bananas and laugh. She tells me to shut up and then finds a card. "This attorney I spoke with, he might be able to help your mom. I told him about the house and he says he'd be willing to talk to her, maybe more. He says half the time simply having an attorney can make things fair. Your mother shouldn't just be tossed out to the street."

"Molly."

She looks up with the sun on her face. She looks so warm right then. "Is that okay?"

"You were in there talking about me?"

Her cheeks flush with her smile. She looks away. "Well, I mean, it came up."

I shake my head.

She sits back. "I told you I'd pay you back."

"No, yeah." I drop my head and laugh. My eyes start watering, but I decide I'm not going to go all Hallmark on her. "I mean, thanks."

We eat in silence for a while. And then, as my refill comes, I sit back, ready to lighten the mood. "Okay, Miss Basketball, who's your team?"

She smiles. "The Lakers."

"Hmm, Lebron, huh?"

"He's so good. He does everything. There is not a single weak spot in his game."

"I would have pegged you for a Warriors fan."

She shakes her head. "I like Lebron. My dad used to scoff. He always said how Jordan was the best. But I like Lebron better. He's so unselfish. Passing, rebounding, he understands the game so well."

I'm slurping up Sprite, smiling. Molly cocks her head. She sets her palms on the table. Her eyes sharpen. "What?" She sits back and throws her hands up. "Oh, yeah, I'm not supposed to know anything about basketball."

"I never said that."

"You know what?" she says, reaching for her purse, counting out some bills. Our waitress hustles over with the bill. "I think I'm ready to show you up. We need to find a basketball court and settle this."

My hand stops, French fry dangling. "Are you being serious right now?"

Molly's eyes widen. "Do I look serious?"

She pulls out some bills to pay for lunch. I wave her cash away. She waves my wave away. "I can pay for my lunch."

I take a glance around, still smiling but wondering. "Molly. What are you trying to prove?"

She stops, two tens in her hand, hovering over the table. "I could ask you that."

"Okay look. We'll find a court on the way home. You beat me, and I'll let you pay me back for lunch."

Our waitress watches as we fight over the money. Molly shakes her head. Her gaze narrows, her smile nothing but confident. Something in those workshops has set a fire in Molly Martinez.

"You drove, paid for gas. You did me a favor by letting me tag along. You will let me pay for lunch."

The waitress shrugs her shoulders, as if to say, *she's got a point.*

I sit back, waving my napkin in surrender. "Be my guest."

It takes forever to get out of the city. Probably because my brain is mush. I make more than a few wrong turns, and we end up crawling behind roughly three thousand trucks. After nearly an hour of looping around, I find Route 29 South, which, eventually will lead us home. I'm in no hurry though, I can't remember the last time I've smiled so much.

I look over to Molly. "Thanks for lunch, by the way."

"You're welcome." She turns to me with a squint. She's got this excellent squint to go with her dimples. Her eyes crinkle, and her nose kind of scrunches while her lips curl with happiness.

I get the Honda up to fifty-eight miles an hour, the sweet spot. Anything over sixty and the steering wheel shakes and the dashboard rattles with all the turbulence under my feet. But fifty-eight is a nice, smooth ride, even as other cars zoom past us like we're sitting still. The car hums along as I start to play the reverend but then figure it's time for something new. I fiddle with the radio, finding an old school rap song I remember one of my elementary school teachers singing in class. We thought it was super lame back then, but later I found the song online and loved it.

I crank the volume and try to keep up with the words to *Parents Just Don't Understand*, nudging Molly and trying to get her into it. I watch her fight it, but then a giggle breaks through and I know I've got her.

Molly shakes her head. "How in the world do you know this song?"

I make a rare lane change to get past an old man in a Buick with bible verses with blocky mailbox stickers stuck to the trunk and bumper. We settle back into the right lane. "I think it was fifth grade. Mr. Evans. He was always singing old rap songs. He said new music was crap and all that. He'd make us listen to this stuff on road trips. He could even breakdance."

She eyes me skeptically. "Breakdance?"

I turn to her to see if she's joking. "Yeah, like..." I jerk my elbow out, trying to do my best robot impression, the best I can do while driving at least. "You know, like, the worm and the backspin?"

She bites her bottom lip, brow wrinkled in confusion. "Um, nope. I think you're going to have to show me."

"Seriously?"

She nods, the look on her face tells me I should seek medical attention.

"How do you not know what breakdancing is?"

"Um, I was born in this millennium?"

"Okay, smarty," I say, slowing down. Molly grips the handle. Her eyes widen and dart around, per usual, but she's still got a wild smile on her face.

"What are you doing?" She checks the side mirror, looks behind us, then to me. I shake my head.

"You need a demonstration."

I find an exit, take another right and drive along looking for a spot. We come up on an empty parking lot, what looks like a rusted-out gas station with stripped out trailers lining the grass around back. The windows are boarded up, covered in swirls of spray paint and graffiti, which only adds to the aesthetics.

Molly's eyes dart around, behind us. "Here?"

"Yep. This is perfect." I crank up the volume as some other old-school hip-hop song comes on the radio. I'm not sure what it is but I'm not about to tell her that. "Put your window down." She does. "Okay, here we go." I shuffle my feet, with no idea what I'm doing. With the gravel and glass it's rough terrain. "I can't really do the worm here."

I set my arms out at my side, my chest convulsing as I do a shake-up then I spin.

It feels good to move after our big day, to release some pent-up energy, and I'm about to hoist Molly out of the car because everything up until now has been movie scene perfect. But then something flashes.

A crunch of gravel as a police car appears, pulling around from the back of the building. It comes gunning past an abandoned carwash bay and it takes me a second to stop dancing and register what's happening. The car jounces over potholes. I leap back. The lights zoom towards us, tires biting for traction as the squad car rounds the turn and slides to a stop directly in front of the Honda.

When the police showed up at parties we'd scatter, just take off running and try to get away then regroup later. But Molly and me, we're just goofing off—dancing—not exactly doing anything wrong. It doesn't matter. Her face flashes from smile to surprise to completely terrified in a blink. It knocks the breath out of me just to see it.

Two officers in the car. The passenger, a bald guy with wraparound sunglasses, puts down his window. "What's going on?"

"What's that?" I say, cupping my ear like a genius. They eye my car. Both cops are younger and look eager to get answers. I glance at my expired inspection, due last month, but I didn't have money for the leak in the exhaust or to fix the crack in the window to get a sticker.

I'm still standing like a robot. I relax, unsure where to go or what to do next. The officer nods at me. "This your car?"

I nod, swallow, and speak. "Oh, yes. Yes, sir."

Molly's gaze shoots back and forth. Her chest heaves as she struggles for breath. Her face is drained, eyes misting while the old school rap song blares. I take a step towards the squad car but the driver steps out and holds up a hand. "Whoa. Just stay right there."

I do as I'm told and stop. I attempt to make a joke, throw my hands up. "I was just having a dance party. My friend has never heard of breakdancing."

The officers exchange looks. The passenger cop steps out of the car. He's stiff and thick and already I can tell he's a complete prick. He's maybe in his late twenties, early thirties. I've played ball with the type. He keeps one hand lingering near his belt. "So uh, have you been drinking?"

"Well, I had some Sprite at lunch. Coffee earlier."

Sometimes I can't help myself. Both cops are out of the car now, grimacing. The driver has a razor sharp buzz cut, hardly looks older than me. The guy doesn't budge. I nod towards the car. "I can turn the music down."

"Go ahead and grab your registration, too," Buzz Cut says.

"Yep."

I lean in the car and kill the music. Molly is nearly having convulsions. Her words come out ragged, breath shaking. "Nat. What's happening?"

"Molly, it's fine," I whisper, going for the glove compartment. But it's not fine, her seat is trembling, her quick breath puffs on my arm. She's radiating fear. "We're okay," I whisper. She wipes her hands on her shorts. I tell her again, under my breath. "Breathe, Molly. Just take it easy."

The officers are out, staring hard. Not hotel security dopes like before, but real live cops with guns and badges. I pop out and make a show of coming out with the registration.

"We were at a convention in D.C., and now we're just on the way home and I needed to dance," I say, like an idiot. I look from cop to cop, Buzz to Baldy. Baldy takes my license and registration back to the car, dispatches flying out the window, traffic slowing to watch the excitement in the lot.

It takes forever, which gives Molly all sorts of time to continue freaking out. It's beginning to freak me out, especially when Buzz nods at my windshield. "Expired inspection."

Buzz approaches, gravel crunching under his feet as he circles the Honda, grunting and nodding. I keep nodding and smiling my best smile for Molly. Even as I fear the worst is coming.

After what feels like hours, Baldy returns, his radio squawking. He hands my license to me and nods to Molly, who's visibly quaking. "Hey there," he says and I'm just waiting for her to scream.

Molly manages a small nod. Baldy turns and faces me again, looks me up and down. "You play ball?"

"Yes," I say, happy to make small talk. "I do. At Woodberry, back home." I nod at my license.

Baldy nods. "Yeah? That's good. Good. Okay, Casablanca, any guy who pulls over to dance, while sober, is all right in my book." He taps the roof of my Honda. "But you need to get this thing inspected, got it?"

I nod and nod and nod, trying not to smile. "Yeah, yes, sir. I will first thing tomorrow. It's actually just an exhaust leak, so I'll—"

Baldy holds up a hand. "Be careful getting home, okay? This isn't exactly a park." He motions over his shoulder. "Had a lot of gang activity around here. Consider this your warning. Get your car inspected, soon. Or maybe just get a new car."

I'm in no position to take offense. More nodding. Happy to be wrong about assuming the guy was a jerk. Speaking of which, Buzz hangs back, looking agitated, like he really wanted to do more here, maybe go through my car, give me a ticket, perhaps haul me into jail to wipe that smirk off my face.

But Baldy is already getting in his cruiser. "Have a good evening."

"You too, sir."

I get in the car, where Molly is sitting on her hands, shivering with panic. Buzz is behind the wheel, still waiting around, watching us closely as I put my seatbelt on and put the car in gear. Molly's breaths come short and fast, she's one blink away from losing it. "It's fine, Molly. It's okay."

Another awkward wave as we get going. I'm ultra-careful to grind the brakes to a complete stop, click my signal, and pull out onto the road only when there isn't a car in sight.

I find the ramp and hit the expressway. The *thump-thump, thump-thump,* of the road the only sound in the car besides Molly's breaths.

"Molly?"

Silence. No radio. No basketball talk. No dimples. She turns to her window. A cloud of fog materializes when she exhales. She turns back to me, her voice low. "That was really, really stupid, you know?"

"Molly. I was just trying to have some fun."

She won't look at me. Only huffs at the window. I sigh and run a hand through my hair. Of course, Molly Martinez can't have any fun. Minutes ago we were happy and light. She was a totally different person. Now, she starts to turn to me but stops. More fog in the window.

The butterflies leave my chest. We put some distance between us and the gas station. It seems stupid to keep worrying about. Sure, it was a close call, but it's over. I want to go back to laughing and having fun. "Look, it all worked out, right? Besides, it's not like I knew the cops were going to show up."

Molly stays at the window with her fog cloud. We drive. And every time she shifts or coughs or sniffles, I look over at her hopefully, thinking she might decide to talk to me, but for nearly an hour she says absolutely nothing. Then, driving south down a stretch of road towards a wall of dark clouds, her head drops and she starts balling.

The balling becomes gasps and soon the gasps are almost choking sobs and she's covering her face and folding over and heaving.

The Honda is again set at fifty-eight, but nothing is smooth anymore. Molly is a mess of tears and terror and hysterics all over again. I thought we could let it go, but apparently, she's been thinking of nothing else this whole time.

I want to reach for her, comfort her, hold her. "We're fine, Molly. We're fine. It's over."

She bolts up straight, shaking her head, wiping her hair. Her voice cracks like glass against a wall. Before I can say anything else, she's screaming at me, smacking her seat. "No it's not, Nat. It's never over!"

The power in her voice jolts me. I glance at her then the road. She shakes her head, her hair falling, her eyes accusing me. "Why did you pull over, why did you do that?"

Her wet glare kills me. She looks ready to slap me, punch me, even.

"Molly."

She rubs her eyes. Her body is coiled tight, her voice strained and stuck in her throat. She shakes her head. "I can't...I can't be around you if you're going to do that. Talking and joking with the police," she says, still shaking her head. Left and right, left and right. It's like she's outside of herself.

"Molly, okay, I got it. We got lucky, I mean, with the inspection. We should be thankful."

"Lucky? *Thankful*." She spits out the words like I'm insulting her.

"Yes. Lucky. *Thankful*." I nod at the windshield. "Not sure if you noticed but I do, in fact, have an expired inspection. And I don't know why you're yelling at me. It wasn't my fault."

She rolls her eyes. Her face is red and splotchy. Another glance out the window, then she turns to me with a whisper. "I didn't say it was your fault. But, why can't you understand?"

"What do you mean?"

"Nat. If that had been me. If...if you looked like me, do you really think we would be driving off, just joking down the road right now?"

"Molly. I had a license. I gave it to them."

"You cannot be this stupid."

"Oh come on, Molly. You don't know that. You don't know them.

Look, you're right. I don't know what your life is like. But at the same time, my life isn't what you make it out to be. You make it sound so, glamorous. It's not. And again, we weren't doing anything wrong."

She throws her hands out as though she's swatting away some imaginary force. "Nat, please. Please try to understand something for once, okay?" She bangs her hands on her seat, wipes her head, and begins to sob all over again. "To them, my whole life is wrong. Don't you get that?"

The rain starts fat and heavy, smacking the windshield before the storm dumps on us. We slog through our misery, the wipers slapping side to side, smearing streaks across the windshield. I slow to a crawl as we approach an overpass where the rain goes silent as I pull off to the side beneath it.

Molly looks at me like I'm crazy.

I shrug. "Look, I can't drive in this. My wipers are crap. I know you might find it hard to believe that a white person doesn't have working wipers, but—"

I stop talking and take a breath. I'm being an asshole. Molly closes her eyes as though transporting herself, and we sit under the bridge and stew. I feel terrible for her, but again, why is she the only one who can have problems? I have all sorts of problems right now.

After a while, when the windshield fogs over and the wind blows the rain in from the back, I try again. This time to point out our similarities and not our differences. "Look, neither of us have a dad, okay? At least you have school. I don't even have that."

It's petty and ridiculous and I'm ashamed of it as soon as it leaves my mouth. For me to compete with Molly's problems. We should be celebrating after the day we've had, but instead we sulk. Molly's anger and fear at ends as she sits with her arms under her legs and her mouth balled up tight.

I attempt to fix the bag in the window for something to do, then try finding a station on the radio, which doesn't happen because we're sitting under a bridge. Sitting with the rain and the fog and the quiet, I give up and turn the wipers off. I push the CD button and let Mazzy Star serenade our melancholy.

The storm rumbles. Cars and trucks slog past. I'm content to stare out at the downpour, even as I realize it's no use, Molly's too good. She wraps herself up in silence like a blanket, gets good and cozy. So after five, ten, fifteen minutes of mutual silence, I'm surprised when Molly pulls her knees to her chin and turns her glossy brown eyes to me.

"My dad worked construction. He was always coming home muddy. Big clumps of dirt like a cast around his boots. My mom always made him take them off outside. I remember staring at them, those enormous boots, the dried red clay, thinking how hard he must have worked to get so muddy."

She turns away. I try to think of something to say but she's not finished. "He worked construction all his life, one job site to the next. But he never got out of the mud." She shrugs. "It never seemed to bother him. He didn't mind. He would work through his shirts, tearing them, sweating them through then washing them until the fabric disintegrated. He was always in jeans, his hard hat and tools always by the door, ready to go. He loved to build things, to fix things. He said it was all he knew."

Molly shakes her head, as though disagreeing with the thought. "That's not true. He loved planes, watching them in the sky. Sometimes we'd go to the airport and watch them take off and land at night. He was fascinated with machines, how things worked. And he loved basketball. He loved to sit on the couch with me, pointing out things you wouldn't see unless you knew what to look for."

"The high-low game, right?"

She nods, a thick rope of tears streaming down her cheeks. "He was never afraid, Nat."

I look over to her, her profile against the wet, blurry window. There is so much love inside of her, so much life and so much more I will probably never know. And so much fear. She lets the tears flow. Her eyes are wet, but her voice is even, back to normal.

I grip the wheel. "So what happened?"

She swallows, sniffs again. "He fell."

"Fell?"

She nods, wiping her eyes. "He was working at the college. They were on the roof at the field house. I don't know much else, only that he wasn't wearing a safety harness. He must have slipped, but he fell and broke his arm and wrist, hurt his back. He went to the hospital. Mom said we couldn't visit him. By then I knew why." New tears flood her eyes. It's all I can do not to wipe them away. Her voice cracks. "I remember thinking he was lucky. We were lucky he didn't die."

I stare straight ahead, to the water dumping from the sky. Molly lets out a breath, wet as the rain, then follows my gaze out the windshield. "So, the owner of the company, he calls and says he's going to take care of everything. He tells my mother he wants to give us some money to tide us over. Mom was hopeful. Dad was happy. He'd been talking to a lawyer about workers comp or something, because he was going to be out for a while. Maybe for good." She stops and swallows. "We thought it was real."

Her mouth goes tight as she steels herself against the emotion. A motorcycle pulls in on the other side and parks. Molly's eyes open and she looks past me, searching. But it's just a guy getting out of the rain. I nod to her. It's okay.

She sits back. "So the next day, my dad hobbles out of our apartment, down the steps and to his truck. He was smiling. I remember it so clearly, even the pain couldn't take his smile as he slid into his truck. He thought this would help, solve our problems. Ashley was two and Mom was pregnant with Ana. And he drove, with a broken arm, wrist, a bad back, and some cracked ribs. He drove right into a trap."

"Wait, what?"

Molly wipes her eyes. "He told me later, over the phone—I haven't seen him since that day, Nat. Three agents were waiting for him as he pulled into the parking lot. It was a setup."

"What, like the owner of the company set it up?"

She shrugs. "I guess. Called immigration. Easier than paying workers comp."

"Damn." I sit back, thinking about these worlds we live in. One with mommy bloggers talking about trips to Disney, LegoLand, contests and giveaways, glitz and glamour and all of those shiny SUV's in a hotel parking lot, and now, looking at Molly, I see a world where a teacher preys on her status, an employer gets his way. I see the fear in her eyes when the cops pulled into the lot, all the helplessness in which she's lived. How she must feel completely invisible.

"See, Nat. It's not that our fathers don't exist. They do. I have a father. He's just not here."

"I know. Look, I'm sorry about what I said, I just, I don't know."

She shakes her head. She sets her hand on mine. "I guess what I'm trying to say is yeah, we both have problems. I'm not arguing with you about who has it worse, okay? I think we're both just trying to exist, you know?"

Exist. Yeah, something like that. I make a fist, tight, but the pain is gone. I miss it, even though I shouldn't. I shouldn't expect pain or enjoy pain. When I start to make a fist again, Molly takes my hand, softly, rubs her fingers on it. This whole time I've been thinking it's me vs. everything. But it's not. I'm not alone.

Molly gives my hand a squeeze. "I'm just trying to exist, Nat."

Maybe it's the rain. The gentle patter of all the water coming off the bridge. Her hand in mine, those big, glossy brown eyes of hers, but when she leans over the console and I lean over some, to where I can feel the warmth of her neck, smell the shampoo in her hair as I rub her hand back, our faces tilt closer. I feel her breath quivering on my lips, closer still, as I lean in to close the last inch between us. But when I go to kiss her, she gasps and pulls away.

I let go of her hand and sit up straight. "Oh um...Molly, I'm sorry."

She blinks, stares at her lap, taking deep, deep breaths. "No, it's okay, I just..."

We both turn away from each other. I look out to the guy with the motorcycle. I can't believe I'm such an idiot. I can't even face her. I talk to my window. "Molly, I'm really, really sorry."

She shakes it off. "No, Nat. It's not, I mean, I want to, but...I'm still, after the other thing, you know?"

"Right. I know, I mean, I don't know why I did...that."

Great, try to kiss a girl spilling her guts to you. *Nice one, Reams.*

3 1

Eventually, the rain lets up. And being how I'm too humiliated to sit under a bridge any longer, I start the car and we plunge ahead. Things are silent again, but it's a new sort of silence. Not our usual comfortable silence and not the sulky silence from before, but the dreaded Awkward Silence. I can't even peek over to her seat.

A few miles later I stop for snacks. Molly waits in the car and when I return, I hand her the water. "I got some chips, a candy bar, and Skittles. Molly, look, I'm really—"

She smiles and shakes her head. "Nat. Stop apologizing."

The rest of the way home Molly flips through pages of notes. She's got numbers to call and people to turn to for answers. I think about Mom, and what's going to happen, what Dr. Wills said to do and how to talk to her and how to go about the school board hearing next week.

The storm clouds are behind us. A reddish sun peaks out for one last go at it. My phone rings. Cora's name comes up. I silence the call.

"You should probably take that," Molly says, eyeing the phone after I've placed it in the console.

"Huh? Why?"

She raises her eyebrows. "Because it's your girlfriend."

"Not my girlfriend. I thought I told you about that."

"Mmm hmm." She gets back to her notes. I laugh. Molly chews on her pen.

"What?"

"I didn't say anything."

I look at her, then the road. It feels like we've spent a week together instead of a day. Not even a whole day. One with plenty of ups and downs. Most of the downs happening on this rainy trip back home. At least that's what I'm thinking when Molly, still staring at her notes, shakes her head. "You can do a whole lot better than Cora Connors, anyway."

"Oh yeah?"

She nods, biting the pen, flipping through pages. I can't help my smile.

It's around seven when we pull into the driveway. The grass needs cutting but otherwise the house looks intact. No smoke or broken windows. Molly gathers her things and finds yet another banana and offers it to me.

"No thanks."

She goes for the handle but then stops and looks at me and laughs. I leap out and get the door and before I can stop myself I blurt it out again. "Look, just let me say this. About the bridge."

"Stop." Molly brushes past me, but then stops and turns and comes back and we're staring at each other, face to face, her eyes softer as her gaze falls to my chest and she steps closer. She takes my hand and my heart launches into a new gear as she smiles and comes closer still, and I take her other hand and I'm trying to think of something to say when the door busts open and Ana and Ash come shooting outside, squealing, "Giant man!"

We break apart. Molly laughs and starts for the porch as the girls shoot past her and run to me. I nod my head and smile triumphantly. Molly rolls her eyes.

I hunch over, hands on my knees. "Hey, short girls."

They slam into me with damp hair and huge smiles. "We went swimming!"

I look at Molly. "Uh, oh yeah?"

"Yeah," Ana says, bouncing. "I was a mermaid."

"I jumped off the diving board," Ashley boasts.

No sign of Mom. Mrs. Martinez steps out on the porch with a desperate look on her face, and my stomach drops. Because I know. I just know.

"That's so awesome," I tell the girls, trying to get my voice behind it. Molly shoots a glance at me and I try my best to hide all the worry racing around inside my head. I set Ana down. I work to keep my voice level. "I'll just, I need to run inside, okay?"

Molly gathers the girls and I don't need to look at Mrs. Martinez's face again. Each step and I see Mom, flushed and drinking, maybe hacking off her hair or...

I barge into the house. "Mom?"

"Back here, honey."

I hurry into the kitchen, steps slowing as I find her on the kitchen floor. My breath catches at the sight of her. Her face is a roasted red, eyes pink and glossy. I stand planted on the floor, waiting for the worst. But it's something different.

No wine glasses. Just her with a bottle of aloe, slathering it on her arms and legs. "Oh, I just got burned right up, Nat."

I laugh, because, well, just because. "Yeah," I say. "Um, where did you guys go?"

"To the club," she says with a wince. "I forgot sunscreen though, ouch."

My shoulders ease back into place. My breath returns to normal. And then I'm laughing harder. "Wait, you took the girls to the swim club?"

"Yeah, where else? We had a delightful time. They wore me right out, though."

Unbelievable. Mom, with Ana and Ashley, marching up the hill to the same pool where I used to have swim practice. Home of the

Beavers. A flash of sun, the whiff of the snack bar hits and I'm nine years old. SUV's and minivans, the team moms and the silent pressure to win the swim meets against the other clubs.

"Mom, we haven't been members there for like three years."

She shrugs, her hair looks like straw, tinged light from the sun, her skin a deep shade of maroon. She rubs aloe into her arm, looking at me over her elbow. "What were they going to do, Nat, call Dan?"

I fall into a chair, shaking my head. Limbs heavy, I'm too drowned by the exhaustion of the day. Mom rolls her neck. "So how was it, did you guys go to the Smithsonian?"

"No, we didn't make it to the Smithsonian."

I never told her, never said a thing to her about what we were doing. She looks up, waiting for more. I shift in my chair to face her, resting my elbows on my knees, hoping I don't start crying or freaking out just when Mom is starting to do so well. I was going to wait to tell her, but now, seeing her face, I can't. "We uh, we may have found some help, Mom. For Molly and her family. For us, too."

Her smile drops. Her eyes cut to me then her gaze is back on the floor. She focuses on the rubbing, breathing through her nose. I should have waited.

"Mom," I duck down. "Mom, we have to face this." *This*, being the house. *This*, being our future. *This*, being her health. There is a lot of *this* in this house.

She nods, slowly. Then, before we get any further, the girls bust into the kitchen.

"Giant. Giant."

Ana leaps into me, and then we are all on the kitchen floor. Mom smelling of Aloe, Ana with her arms around my neck and Ashley dancing around me. I squeeze my eyes shut before I glance up to find Molly and her mother at the counter. And they probably think we're loons, but the smiles on their faces say they're okay with us being loons.

32

Later, when Molly and the girls are off to bed, I listen to the animated hum of Molly's voice as she reads, the girls asking questions and Molly's patient, thoughtful responses. Exhaustion hits as I make my rounds through the house, turning off lamps, stopping in the kitchen for water before checking Mom's room where I find a familiar lump on the bed, only this time done in by sun and fun and not drinking. I shut the door quietly, find the couch, and get back to my new favorite hobby.

Dr. Wills' website has a MEDIA section, a BOOKS section, and an ABOUT section. There are pictures of her with all sorts of important people. Congresswomen. Authors. Distinguished men in tuxedoes and wire framed glasses. Intellectual types clutching their own books. It also has a BLOG section. And Dr. Wills has been busy, because there's a new post as of an hour ago.

What Matters Most

I sit up, my heart catching.

I'm at the Her Turn *convention in the nation's capital, along with several of the world's leading bloggers. It's been a huge success and a* lot of fun, as expected. I've met so many new people and caught up with many colleagues, but it was something unexpected that's weighing on my mind tonight. Something that shook me up and got my attention.

I'd just finished presenting, speaking in a conference room. It wasn't great, and I am not ashamed to admit feeling more than a little bit sorry for myself. The new book isn't coming along and the old one isn't exactly flying off the shelves. It happens, it's part of the business. But sometimes, it's a drag.

Yes, it is true. Even psychiatrists get the blues. But I was doing my best to give my best when I found a face near the back of the room. A young man's face with charming but pained blue eyes, eyes that grew intense as he sat forward, seemingly hanging on my every word.

Something about his passion. How he was sitting at an almost empty table, a book bag at his feet, I can't say exactly, but suddenly, I wasn't going through the normal talk of parenting and mental health, I was speaking to him.

I didn't remember him being back there when I'd come on, but as I spoke about parenting and mental health, I watched his face soak it up (the kid took notes!). Finishing up, as he stood to leave, I was almost calling him out and begging him to stay. I nearly chased after him (no offense to the wonderful ladies who stayed back to talk with me).

This kid stayed in my mind, and yes, the longer he stayed the more he became Ben. His focus, his intentions, the circumstances that had brought him there. Sure, he could have been with his parents, but something told me he needed to talk.

And then he returned.

He walked in, looking nervous and disoriented but nevertheless determined. He took a seat at a table near the front. And just like that, I was convinced he was why I'd decided to come here and speak. Clichéd yet true, he was the reason I was there.

So then it was my turn (ha!). I sat down beside him. For this post, we'll call him "Mike."

Mike was tall with curly brown hair and those sad eyes. The only other thing I'll say about his physical description, he has a wonderful smile. We got through the pleasantries and then he said something that really got to me.

Mike said he felt like I was speaking about his mother. His home.

Well, truthfully it was all I could do not to break down. He didn't even know who I was, he'd wandered in for other reasons, and for his benefit, I will not say.

And he was seventeen.

Ben would have been seventeen this year.

And it was like I was staring at my own son. As though Ben had come back to me, just for a moment, to ask me to fix this. Trying to compose myself, I gave Mike my information. I offered my services. I did everything but beg him to let me help.

Later, we took a stroll around the block, and talking to this kid was a humbling experience. He had driven up for a friend, for her benefit, because Mike was a real friend. He's having issues at school, at home, and everywhere in between. But Mike, all is not lost.

If you're blog stalking (I have a feeling you are), know that I'm rooting for you. We can do this. I am a lawyer, an author, and yes, a doctor. But most importantly I am a mother. I will always be a mother.

-MW

I read it five or six times, thinking about our walk, our talk, even such delusions as fate or chance. Whatever brought Molly and me together, Dr. Wills to the convention, it all seems tied together. I just need to figure out a way to sort it out and make it work.

I start to leave a comment but stop myself. I lay back on the couch, letting the day roll me over. I'm through taking action for now. Through thinking about Mom and the house and if she's ready to let it all go and start over. I just let it slip away. I let it go and let the exhaustion come over me.

And eventually I fall asleep on the couch.

Mom is up early, griping about her sunburn. I yawn and stretch then figure I might as well give it another shot.

"So, Mom." I begin slowly, feeling things out. "At the convention, I uh, I met a lawyer, someone who could contact the bank and look into our um, situation."

She turns and looks me over. "I thought you were helping Molly?"

"I was. I am. We are. I just, well, I met someone who might be able to help us, too."

She gets back to scrubbing, then turns back to me again. "Like with your board hearing?"

"Well, yeah, with that." I'm almost surprised to hear her say it. My hearing, it sends pangs into my chest. "But also, I mean, about our situation. We have to talk about this tax thing, you know?"

I wait for her to pull back, lash out, fling the soap from her hands and tell me she can't deal with it. It's what Mom does. She avoids, deflects, blames, shuts herself off with her own delusions. But not this time. This time she wipes her eyes with the back of her wrist and sets her hands at the sink to steady herself. This time she drops her head.

I take a breath and wait. Still waiting for it to come. The usual griping about my dad or Herndon or whoever else she's come up with to blame. Instead, she turns to me, tears streaking down her cheeks to her quivering lips. She takes my face in her wet hands. "Nat. I'm sorry."

I shake my head. I place my hands on her wet, soapy hands. A surge of tears hit my eyes. "No Mom, it's fine."

"It's not fine. I've been terrible. Really, really terrible. I know that."

The guilt takes hold of her face. It contorts her mouth, her lips, how her chin scrunches up and she shakes and I blink and blink harder because it might be worse than her tantrums. But then she brings me in and squeezes me tight, tighter than she's squeezed me in a long time, and with her warm dishwater palms on my back, her tears soaking through the front of my shirt, I set my arms around her and realize the guilt has me too. And I'm too tired to hold it in any longer.

"Oh sweetie," she says in between muffled sobs. "I'm so sorry."

I hold her again as she cries. We cry, and after a while I stop worrying whether Mrs. Martinez is at work or about who might stroll in and see us bawling out on an otherwise sunny Sunday morning. When I let her go she wipes her nose and nods, still nodding her head as she looks me in the eyes. "I'm ready to try, you know? I can't promise anything but I'm ready to try."

I can't help my eyes leaking new tears because it's the most honest thing she's ever said. "Yeah Mom. That's okay, yeah."

33

On the morning of my board hearing, Mom and I have breakfast together. Bacon, eggs, and toast for me, yogurt for her. I sneak peeks her way, at her clear eyes, her small smile. She asks how I'm feeling, this being Tuesday, the day I've been dreading for so long. She's remarkably sober, sharp, well rested, and even her hair has a healthy shine to it. It's like she's decided to go all out for her role as Mom.

I've told her everything. About Meyers, Molly, what I did. What I think is going to happen. And yet, I'm surprised by my pregame nerves, but I guess it's normal considering my entire future lies in the hands of a five-member board. I spent yesterday at the park, on the basketball court, shooting jumpers until my arms were rubber. Shot after shot, working out the kinks, the rust, the problems and answers. Two hundred jump shots. Then a hundred more. When I got back the house was quiet. Molly took the girls to a movie. I was asleep before they got home.

Things get quiet between Mom and me. She's nursing her yogurt, while I'm finishing up the last of the bacon. I wipe my mouth. I still have a lot to do so I slip out from my chair and walk to the sink when Mom slides her chair out too.

"Nat, I was thinking. What if we just sell the house, pay the money?"

I turn and look at her, blink my eyes and search for the words. She waves her hand around the kitchen. "We don't need all this space, or the ridiculous rules." She lowers her head. "Or the memories, for that matter. Maybe we could get a little house over in Tenbridge? Near the college." She starts for a sip of coffee but stops short. A small smile curls her lips. "Well, not too little. The girls would need a backyard and…"

I set the plate in the sink, waving my hands to stop her, trying to keep up with all of this. "Hang on, hang on. Slow down for a minute. The girls?"

"Yes, I've grown quite fond of them. Especially Ana, what an angel."

My mouth opens, shuts. Maybe Mom has a vision of the girls roaming a field of flowers. "Are you serious? Do you know what you're saying?" I look back at the closed door to their wing, lowering my voice. "Mom, it's a little more complicated than that."

"Oh, well, you and Molly, right? We need to set some ground rules for the two of you, but—"

I nearly leap away from her. "No, no. Mom stop. Not at all what I mean."

On cue, the door opens, and there stands Mrs. Martinez in her hotel uniform. She looks surprised to see us in the kitchen, and I must look crazy, hunched over, wide-eyed and gawking at my Mom. Molly is behind her mother, her eyes locked in on me. "Oh, good morning," I say to them, backing away from Mom, Mr. Casual now.

Molly, in her baggy long sleeve and jogging pants, hands fidgeting, steps into the kitchen, still looking at me but now with the hint of a smile. "Can I talk to you?"

I nod like crazy, wondering what else this day has in store.

Mom and I drive downtown in silence. I find a place to park about a block away and it gives us some time to walk. She takes my arm in her frail hand. She's too skinny, her shirt hangs loose. Out in the world, she looks fragile, her cheeks almost gaunt in the sunlight, but I can't worry about it right now. She's here, she's trying, and that's all I can ask.

We stop at the stairs to the admin building. Mom turns to me, taking my hands. "Nat, whatever happens..."

I shake my head, glance up the stairs towards the worn bronze doors of the admin building. "Mom."

She reaches for my hair, moves my bangs around. "No, listen. I'm proud of you, okay. I'm not proud of myself, but I am so very proud of you. Not just for this, but for everything."

"Thanks, Mom." I look around. "I'm more worried about Molly."

Mom smiles. "You're too young to worry."

"You're never too young to worry, right?"

I'm trying to make a joke but Mom only blinks. I look down to the marble steps. My feet hurt because dress shoes are too narrow.

Inside, the old tile floors are worn and beige from use. People mill around, stretched out on the cushioned benches, leaning against the worn cinderblock walls. I spot DeShaun and the guys lining the wall. A quick swell of adrenaline emerges, what I used to feel before we took the court during away games.

Coach Taylor approaches with a grimace-smile he reserves for these little coaching moments. He sets a hand on my shoulder. "You hanging in there, Nat?"

"Yes, sir." I'm tempted to snap, say, *Sure, thanks for having my back all this time, Coach.* But I've left it behind, the blame, the anger, the...worry. It's all out on those steps. It's gotten me nowhere I needed to be. I guess it's time to move on, ahead, get this thing settled. Besides, he's here now, and that's something.

DeShaun comes up and wraps me up in a bear hug. We break apart and I give him a quick shove. "Just like your defense."

"My man." He shakes his head, eyeing me like I've been lost at sea. DeShaun has this cool scar just above his right eyebrow, a nasty elbow he caught in the face freshman year. I was there, and it was gruesome when it happened, the gym went silent as he writhed in a pool of blood under his face, his feet kicking on the floor. I remember rushing over to him and seeing the gash to the bone. Now it's faded, almost silvery. He's sort of grown into it.

Most of my teammates have shown up. One by one they come in and we slap hands. They all say how they wished they'd known. A few of them are younger guys, ones I don't know too well. But it's nice either way, having them around.

A plan is in action. I mostly know what to expect—what I hope to expect anyway—but behind the wooden doors, hearing the rumble of the decision makers, I'm not so sure anymore. My feet are like ice as Coach checks his watch. "Well, I guess we better get inside."

DeShaun slaps my back as the doors creak open and we enter. Inside, it's already hot and stuffy. With all of us basketball players pouring in, things get really cramped. The first tingle of sweat finds my neck.

It's really nothing more than a glorified office space, with worn, threaded carpet with the fading WCS logo in the middle. Wood paneling covers the walls behind the five board members hovering over microphones.

Mom and I find a place against the back wall as a frazzled lady with gray, frizzy hair lays into the board about the stress of her profession and the stagnant teaching pay scale.

Up front, a screen shows a timer like a scoreboard in a basketball game. Each public speaker is given three minutes to plead their case, and this teacher lady is making the most of things. It's clear she's armed with facts, her voice firm and powerful, shaking the room. When she gets worked up her arm brushes the microphone and the little podium wobbles. I glance at Deshaun, who cocks his eyebrows. Who knew these board meetings were so intense?

The teacher lady has some support behind her, a few whistles and cheers when she cites the numbers. She's making less than she was in 2013, she says, which according to her was a piss poor wage to start. The board chairman, Dr. Krise according to his nameplate, takes offense at her "vulgarities" as he calls them. It doesn't look like the teacher really cares, though.

The board members have taken notice of us in the back, probably because nine lanky basketball players are hard to miss. There are some creaks and shuffling as those in attendance swivel around, and by the time the teacher finishes ripping the board and shuffles her papers, my heart is banging away. A quick glance around. I don't see Mr. Meyers but I spot Virgil squeezed into a seat near the wall. He's even taken off his hat. His hair is combed over and he's trimmed his beard. He gives me a sheepish wave. I smile and nod my thanks.

"Next speaker, please."

It's six twenty-six when a tiny girl tucks her hair behind her ears and tips to the podium. She walks head down, timid, her nervousness almost palpable as she cranes her head to speak into the microphone.

"I'm Wendi Chalmers," she stammers, hardly able to get her name out. "I'm a sophomore at Garner High."

Immediately I feel both sorry for and proud of her. She's obviously terrified, but whatever she's up here to discuss means enough to her to face it. She straightens some papers out in front of her and clears her throat.

"I'd like to address the safety procedures at our school. In light of the recent shootings in Texas, I think it is time to put some procedures in place." She stops, stutters, wipes her hair back and breathes. I'm cheering her on from inside my head. *Do it, Wendi, you can do it.*

With a shaky voice, she describes a lockdown last year. I remember it, too. There had been some online threats and everyone was sort of sketched out, but the police wouldn't share anything with the students. All we knew were the rumors, as Wendi discusses now. I remember thinking, wondering what it would look like, who it would be to storm up the stairs into the lobby and pull out a gun and start blasting away. The news trucks rushing in, the helicopters flying overhead, all of us in the parking lot, hugging and guessing.

We shouldn't have to worry about that, Wendi tells the board, her voice catching steam. "*You* didn't have to worry about this. *You* have no idea what it's like to sit in a class, the door open and vulnerable, wondering when you're going to hear the crack of gunfire. We do. *We* worry about it every time we see it in the news. That is why *we...*" she stops here, just as she's finding her groove.

"Tell 'em, Wendi." DeShaun urges. Coach glares at him. Wendi halfway turns her head, nods her thanks. It seems to give her the strength she needs to finish. She looks up from her notes.

"It's why I'm here, in hopes that you will see. So that you will take action before it's too late."

"Thank you, Miss Chalmers."

We burst into applause. The whole place does. I'm clapping so hard my hands hurt. Wendi glances at us and sort of bows her head, then she hurries back to her seat, her face bright red and looking hot enough to burn.

It's time. And I'm nearly shaking, nervous, even though this is nothing more than procedure. Meyers is nowhere to be found, neither is Molly.

"Next on the agenda," an obviously unmoved Dr. Krise begins. I work my breathing, taking in slow, deep breaths to lower my pulse. "Nathanial Reams."

He looks up. "Is Mr. Reams present?"

Mom squeezes my hand. I suck a breath and walk to the podium, forcing myself to greet them head on. DeShaun slaps my back again. Here we go.

"Mr. Reams," Dr. Krise begins.

At the podium, I have to lean down to speak into the microphone. "Yes, sir," I say, finding my voice and a newfound respect for what

Wendi just did. All those eyes on me, boring into my back, the sides of my face.

Dr. Krise shuffles some papers. His white hair and black glasses are something from a history book. I wonder if he thinks the bow tie makes him look dignified. It doesn't. It makes him look like Colonel Sanders. But he's about to announce my fate, so I hold my eyes to his and ready myself for whatever they've decided.

Dr. Krise clears his throat, looks at his colleagues, then back to the room. "So, this is a rather, uh, unusual case," he says, jowls swinging. "But from what we have here, what we've learned today, it appears some new evidence has come to light. This evidence—once verified let me add—uh, may change things quite a bit, here."

My insides erupt. I keep my face still. Dr. Krise clasps his hands, gearing up for a sermon. "Mr. Reams. I'll be clear. Nothing discovered today changes the fact that you assaulted a faculty member, on school grounds, no less."

Really? All this time I'd thought I would have been better off jacking up Meyers behind a bowling alley. I keep my emotions in check, knowing if I give them anything, from an eye roll to an outburst, they'll go through with my expulsion. More paper shuffling from Krise. "That said, a student has come forward. It seems the matter is more complicated than first thought."

His fellow board members shift in their seats, probably secretly bemoaning the fact this guy is the spokesperson. Now it's a smile I'm holding back. Because Molly has set this day on fire. This morning, when she hit me with the news, how she and two lawyers were coming forward to force a preemptive meeting, she was so excited she could hardly breathe.

Excited for *me*.

Dr. Krise continues with the formalities, but it's clear things have changed. The team is moving around behind me, some chatter in the board room. I plant my big toe into the carpet, forging it into the floor to keep myself still. "Well, we had a get-together, and decided this will need further looking into."

I'm still waiting on the words. The words I need to hear. Molly said it was going to happen but until it does, I can't quite believe it's true. Now, in this crowded boardroom, growing restless with anticipation, I'm barely hanging on. Every breath in the room hits my neck. And for some reason, I'm thinking about Mom, and how she's trying to turn things around. About Molly, and how even this hasn't destroyed her. And now it's my turn. It's my turn to stay on my feet when everything is coming at me head on, trying to knock me down.

Dr. Krise seems to relish the moment, the wait, as he takes the scenic route to get to the point. "With this new information, it is our decision that for now," he pauses on for now, then waves his hands to the board members. "You be readmitted, pending your—"

The team bursts into cheers. I let my head drop, willing myself not to cry, but it feels like I've been released from a hole in the ground. Dr. Krise's microphone screeches as he takes it in his hand and urges the room to quiet, looking around for a gavel.

The little scoreboard thing has been turned off. I feel the shifting behind me. I take a breath. "Thank you, sir." No one hears me. And the doctor isn't finished pointing at me.

"Pending that, you, as I said, there is still the matter of your exams, your grades. All of this is still preliminary," he says, stressing he can rip the rug from under my feet at any moment.

The benches squeak. DeShaun is laughing. My mom is crying. The board, everyone in the room, rises to their feet, ready to break out into the evening and feel the sunshine while it's still around. I turn and find Mom, Deshaun, the rest of my teammates. Everyone is grabbing and fussing over me.

And all I want to do is go find Molly.

Later

I zip my jacket as fans and parents exit the gym. It's a week before Christmas and winter is right on schedule. I've always loved this time of year. The holidays, winter breaks, tournaments and practice. School is out, and it's the time of year when the day is better spent inside a gym

Leaning against the cold bricks, I check my phone. Nothing from Mom. She usually sends a text asking me to pick something up at the store or maybe just some cute pic of her and whatever the girls are into. I scroll through a few texts from an assistant coach at Roanoke College. The ones I've read hundreds of times. It's weird being recruited again, after being written off and forgotten for so long.

The moon is out when the door swings open and Molly strolls outside, still in her gym shorts, her long sleeve *Garner Basketball* shirt swallowing her whole. Her dimples deepen when she sees me waiting, but her shoulders droop with mock disappointment. "I can't believe I missed those free-throws."

I pocket my phone and kick off the wall. "Yeah, well, we're shooting a hundred on Saturday."

"I know, I know. At least we still won."

I nod my head. Sherri Andrews and Stacey rush out the doors and hug Molly. "Undefeated baby."

Molly with friends. She's always looking up because she's the shortest player on the team. Her eyes still scan her surroundings—probably what makes her such a good point guard—but Molly knows she's not suddenly in the clear of her legal hurdles. Still, a smile blooms across her face. A few high fives. I wait for her teammates to pass, and I quietly bring her in for a hug.

"I think you might make all district."

She shakes her head, shoves away from me playfully. "Right."

"No, seriously. It's not about how much you score, you're a facilitator. A true point guard. Even if you can't make free throws."

Molly slaps me in the gut and I fold over.

"Hey, don't hurt him. We need that guy tomorrow night." DeShaun saunters over, all smiles and swagger. I straighten up and smile. DeShaun nods at Molly. "Nice game."

"Thanks," she says. "*Someone* thinks I need to work on my free throws."

"Yeah?" DeShaun says, hooking a thumb at me. "This dude is trying to coach, now?"

"No," I shake my head, smiling for no other reason but to smile.

DeShaun raises his brow, his gaze lingering on me as he heads into the gym, filing past the people coming out. "See you at practice tomorrow."

Through the shouts of *nice game* and *way to go*, Molly and I make our way towards the car. I walk fast, in a hurry, still not quite able to go a day without the little lump in my chest. But it's getting better, each day I worry a little less.

I get the door, gently because the new window in the back keeps slipping off track. Molly flops into her seat. The Honda cranks then catches. "We've got to hurry if we're going to rescue my mom."

"I think she'll survive."

"I don't know, I could hear the munchkins in the background. It's a mutiny." I think how far Mom has come. She's working part-time and loving it. She's still drinking but not as much. She's talking to a therapist. Her days off are spent with Ashley and Ana. Field trips and lesson plans. She's spoiling them rotten. Best of all, she's trying.

Molly sets her face to the sky. I fiddle with the radio. It's a short drive to our little house, the rental sitting a block from the Woodberry campus. The streets are narrow and the yard is smaller, but there is no homeowners' association, no memories of my dad, and maybe most importantly, no holes in the wall.

I'm through punching things. Walls, trees, teachers.

Technically, my case is pending, but lately there's been talk of time served. I was able to take my exams, pass them, and move on from the dumpster fire that was my junior year. Coach Taylor is talking to small colleges, like Roanoke, doing what he can, as he says. And I'm content to wait it out and see what happens. But I'm still set on Woodberry.

Meyers is on leave, which helps some. But I've found there's a stigma that comes with punching a teacher, despite the circumstances. To some I'll always be a raging psycho, a maniac, a delinquent, or just a dumb jock. Although a few people have called me a hero.

Mostly, people just like to talk. They like to talk about Molly and me living together and what we might be doing. I take it all in stride. Because I'm okay. I'm okay with whatever titles come my way. I know the truth. I'm not a psycho and I'm not a hero. Being a hero takes courage. And I've had a front row seat to a show of courage for the past year.

The Honda scrapes the street as we pull into the small driveway. I haven't even stopped the car before Molly leaps out and rushes to the mailbox, just like she does every day. I keep telling her it's a little early for acceptance letters to go out, but I don't think she hears me over the scream of opportunity in her head. It's great to see her this way, her eyes focused, her head up, the dimples deep and her shoulders squared. Molly is ready to face the world.

Molly is still cautious, but now she's determined to fight. She has the strength, the legal support, the sliver of hope she needed all along. She refuses to be crushed by the system. It's a sight to see.

It's weird. Beautifully weird, all of it. Molly, her mom, the two little girls. All of us together. To some it sounds complicated, but it isn't. It's easy. There's hope in this new house. Enough hope to lead us out of the shadows and into the sunlight. For them, for Mom and me. For our demons.

And maybe that's enough.

ACKNOWLEDGMENTS

What a journey for this book. I finished a version, then scrapped it, finished a different one and scrapped that. I sent another draft to #pitmad where I received some invaluable feedback. With each rewrite the book improved, but something was missing.

Then Molly Martinez arrived, quietly at first, but a force all the same. Strong, smart, and capable, once Molly and Nat's worlds collided I had myself a book. We hear so much about immigration—the politics, the border, the policies—that sometimes it's hard to think about the individual lives involved.

Thanks and love to my mom, an ER nurse, (And no, Mom, Nat's mother is not based on you! Well, maybe the good parts). So many times I watched my mom come home exhausted, only to do it all over again. Shift after shift of trauma, then she'd have to deal with my little brother and me on top of all that.

Big thanks to all the early readers, especially Sarah Miller, who read over many drafts and offered so many suggestions. This book would have never made it without you. To a few unnamed agents out there, who considered the early versions of this book, declined, but were nice enough to give me feedback, praise, advice, and most of all, hope.

To the usual suspects. The Immortal Works Team. Thank you always to Staci Olsen, again and again for all that you do. Thanks to Holli Anderson, for all the red ink. For making all of my stories much better stories. You guys are the best.

Thanks to all my hangouts in the writing world. The prompts, the forums, the comradery of such a relentless pursuit. To Dad, Diane, and Nana for all the encouragement.

Lastly, to the fam. To Simon and Bella and my wife Anne. Thanks for coping with my crazy.

S. A. (Pete) Fanning is the author of *Justice in a Bottle* and *Runaway Blues*. He lives in Virginia with his wife, son, baby girl, and two very spoiled dogs. He can be found at www.petefanning.com, where he's posted over 200 flash fiction stories.

This has been an
Immortal Production

www.ingramcontent.com/pod-product-compliance
Lightning Source LLC
Chambersburg PA
CBHW050852190726
48286CB00007B/2336